I0547286

The Black Rose Banker

by

Bert Entwistle

blackmulepress.com

Books by Bert Entwistle

The Drift
Jack Bannister mystery #1

Uranium Drive-In
Jack Bannister mystery #2

The Taylor Legacy,
An American Family Saga

New Mexico,
A Novel of the Old West

The Black Rose Banker

Murder in the Dell

Leftover Soldiers,
Book 1, Life on the Western Frontier

Leftover Soldiers,
Book 2, Aftermath & Opportunity

Looking Back,
Stories of Real American Pioneers

The Black Rose Banker

Published by Black Mule Press

First published November, 2014
Revised edition, 2023
Phone # (719)-287-8063
Email: westernimages@msn.com

Library of Congress Control Number: 2915916083

ISBN 978-0-9896761-3-7

Author photo, Donald R. Kallaus

Front cover original art by: Andree Ferguson

Price: $12.00

To my friends Jess Knight, Dan Feltner,
Gary Haynes and Dave Pylypczuk.

Author's note:

This story is my first novella sized book for those that like shorter reads but still love a good mystery.

The *Black Rose Banker* is a tale about a brilliant, beautiful young woman who moves around the country assuming new identities as she goes. With each new identity she takes a job with a new business. Within a few months she leaves them to find they have been robbed and one or more of the men have been seduced and murdered.

Working in Colorado as a banker, she meets her match in an FBI Agent driven to find her. Follow the fun as the chase begins.

SECTIONS

"To Sherlock Holmes she is always *the* woman. I have seldom heard him mention her under any name. In his eyes she eclipses and predominates the whole of her sex."

Dr. Watson — A Scandal in Bohemia

The Crime

"Good Christ almighty, a Hollywood script writer couldn't make up a crime scene this horrible." Jack West watched as the well-dressed man in the FBI windbreaker walked slowly through the lobby pulling on black latex gloves and shaking his head in disbelief as he went. Cash and papers mixed in with the blood and the bodies. The odor of death was already evident. "Good Christ Almighty," he repeated again to no one in particular.

The ancient green carpeting soaked it up like a cheap sponge, rapidly turning parts of the floor to a coagulated greenish paste. Blood was everywhere, it stained every counter top, wall and chair. Small trickles ran slowly down the plastic lens of the fluorescent light fixture above the teller station. When the blood reached the corner of the fixture, small drops broke free falling on an overturned trashcan, creating a delicate pattern on the plastic.

Looking up, he noticed the man watching him from a small private office. The sign on the door said *Facilities Engineer*. Walking through the door the FBI Agent spoke to the man. "You involved in this mess?"

Jack West was tall and slim, with thin gray hair in need of a trim, wire rim glasses and a thick bushy moustache. His look was more like that of a cowboy, which he had been in his earlier years, than a city guy. He leaned back in the chair, just touching the wall. It was about the only place he could find without bloodstains.

"I guess I'm responsible for part of it," he said, sticking his hand out to grip the agent's. "Jack West, Rampart Bank security."

"Bert Deverou, Special Agent, FBI, tell me about it."

"Running his fingers through his hair, West closed his eyes and started to recall the events leading up to the shootout. Taking a long drink from a Mountain Dew, he prepared himself to replay the morning's events. He began slowly, the stress of the day showing deeply on his face. "I work for bank security. I was brought in undercover by our Minneapolis office three and a half months ago," he said, pausing a moment to help clarify the sequence in his mind. "As you guys know, there have been several takeover robberies in Colorado in the last year, two of them, now three of them I guess, have been Rampart Bank operations."

"You said undercover?"

"Yeah, they set me up as their maintenance man, a good cover actually. It allowed me to go everywhere and no one suspected anything." While the FBI man made notes in his book, West took another sip from the can, now getting warm on the desk.

"Jack, can you give me the sequence of events in short form, we'll get back to the details later."

"Sure. It started about seven fifteen this morning. The Rocky Mountain Certified Transport truck pulled up in front just like every day. The manager went to the door and let the blonde headed guard come in with a two wheeler. Everything looked like a normal day until he came out of the vault."

Deverou interrupted his train of thought. "Did you see a gun come out at this point?"

"Not right away," said West. "I was behind the back counter. I didn't suspect anything until the guard started screaming out orders and people started diving for cover." The scene came crashing back in vivid technicolor, he couldn't stop thinking about it even if he tried.

"When I looked up, he had a revolver in his right hand. A stainless Ruger model GP100, .357 mag." West continued nonstop, "I have a blue model of the same pistol at home. He ordered everyone down. When the new guy, Anthony, didn't move he put one round above his right eye. A hollow point, judging from the blood and brains on the wall."

Before Deverou could interrupt, Jack took a quick breath and spoke again, not missing a beat in his narrative.

"When he went down, I pulled my gun and touched one off at the blonde guard. It knocked him down, but the damn vest saved his ass." On a roll now, he had trouble getting out the words as fast as the pictures moved through his mind.

"The other guard came in the front door and pulled out his gun, but he seemed unclear about what to do next. That's why I'm not sure about his part in this. At any rate," said West, finally beginning to catch his breath, "he stepped in my line of fire and caught one just off the edge of the vest. Have you heard how he's doing?"

"They say he'll recover, but he's got a lot of questions to answer before he leaves the hospital." He looked up from his notebook, "What about the blonde guard, did you hit him more than once?"

"Three more times, twice in the vest and one I think went through the upper left arm or shoulder."

The FBI agent sat quietly, hardly believing what he heard. "And the other two dead? Who killed them?"

"The blonde guard started shooting at everyone that moved. That's when the assistant manager got hit and the janitor ran for the door. He was a new guy named Eddie, he just stopped in to check on supplies, he got it in the back."

"Jack, just how the hell did the blood get on the ceiling?"

"That's the assistant manager's, Sandy Klarke. She was a nice lady; her son is a local Police Officer. The guard was on his back shooting up at her. The slug caught her square on the chin and went out through the top of her skull."

"And then what happened to the guard?"

"The scumbag managed to get up and out the door with one money bag, and left in a small red hatchback car with temporary tags. I don't know what kind. I just realized; it must have been parked here already; the armored truck is still here . . ."

"What's your take on this? How many do you think are involved?"

"Right now I'd say two, possibly three. The blonde guard obviously, and the other guard in the hospital, and maybe even a driver, I'm not really sure."

Making a few more notes, Deverou asked West for the manager's name.

"Winter Day," said West.

Deverou looked up at West, "Winter Day? Are you serious about that name?"

"Serious as those dead bodies. Winter Day is her name. However, before I start in on her, I need some fresh air. This lady is a book all by herself."

Bert Deverou, sixty-five years old on his last birthday, thought he'd seen just about everything. Even with two tours in Southeast Asia with the Special Forces, ten years in the Secret Service, personal bodyguard for many high profile people and now the FBI. He'd never seen this kind of abject and senseless violence until today.

The tiny corner office was badly in need of paint and carpet, much like the rest of the branch. West's space didn't show much evidence of occupation, a desk, two chairs, one 2 drawer file cabinet and a computer were just about the only sign of use. A few papers, a small empty vase and a group picture of the staff at a Christmas party were all that disturbed the scene.

"I'm with you," said Deverou. "We could both use a little fresh Colorado air right now." Walking through the lobby with the FBI agent, Jack still couldn't believe the carnage all around him. Crime scene people were everywhere. Even when the bodies are removed they would have days of work in front of them.

*

Glad to be out the door, they were confronted by a sea of police, fire and ambulance lights and an even larger army of press. The TV cameras and reporters were pressing the yellow crime scene tape tighter and tighter and the police had all they could do to keep them back.

The bank sat at the end of a huge Mall parking lot, a tired looking example of late seventies design covered with green and gray tile's on the outside that were drab and dirty. When the politicians and lobbyists managed to get branch banking voted in, the mom and pop operations were soon bought up by the big chains, and the big chains were bought by the giant banking concerns. Today, the Meadowgate branch had been part of merger after merger and looked much worse for the wear. Years of poor maintenance and poor security practices, by companies more concerned with profit than people, made it a vulnerable target for theft from inside and out. That's why West was hired, to look at things from a working branch level and see where improvements were needed. The need for improvements became crystal clear today.

West watched while Deverou continued writing his notes, thinking how much he looked like the poster child for an FBI recruiting poster. Tightly cropped brown hair just turning gray, neat dark suit, plain red tie and polished black wingtips. An American flag pin was on his left lapel. Even his notebook looked formal, with the Bureau's logo stamped on it. *All these guys seemed to be little J. Edgar Hoover's*, thought West.

Deverou walked into the small trailer serving as the bureau's mobile command center. After issuing instructions to several other agents he turned back to West. "Jack, let's talk about the armored car guys and Winter Day."

"The armored car company supervisor is on his way with the guards files," said West, "We'll know more about them when he gets here. As for Winter, I can't really believe she's involved in this deal. She does have a pretty unique history, but still, it's doesn't look like something she would be involved with."

Making more notes in his book, Deverou asked, "How long have you known her?"

"I first met her at another branch, after she transferred to Colorado Springs from Fairplay, Colorado, maybe three months ago," said West.

"When did you start to suspect her?"

The question took him by surprise, "I didn't say I suspected her of anything," said West, locking eyes with Deverou. "But she did change when she started at this branch. At the downtown branch she dressed very conservatively. Everything she wore was long pants, long dresses and long sleeves, completely buttoned up." He recalled the first time he saw her on the teller line, "I guess you might say she was kind of nondescript. After she transferred here, she started to change. Miniskirts, spike heels and revealing clothing were her norm."

Deverou tapped his pen on the notebook, as though digesting and sorting all this new information.

West noticed that even the pen was official issue, with the logo printed on it.

"Do you think she was working with the guards to rob this branch?"

"Well I suppose anything's possible, but I really doubt it. Although, I did see a picture once of her and the blonde guard mugging it up in front of the armored car, guns out and everything, kind of Bonnie and Clyde like," said West. "However, that's a long way from her being involved in murder and bank robbery."

"Do you know where she's at now?"

"All I know is everyone but me went to the hospital, that is those of us still alive."

"Where was she when the shooting started?" asked Deverou.

"She was in the cash room, a smaller room inside the vault the whole time. She let him in the front door and led him into the vault right away."

"Jack, I'm confused here, did she let him in the vault without question? Is that procedure?

"Seems to be. After the bankers get to know the guards, they let them have access without question."

Deverou looked puzzled. "It seems like pretty lax security procedures to me."

"I imagine the people coming to claim the bodies will feel the same way," said West, sounding more sarcastic than he really meant to be.

"Do we have tapes from the cash room?"

"No, believe it or not, there aren't any cameras in the most sensitive place in the bank."

Deverou just shook his head. "I guess we better find Miss Day and have a little talk."

*

West handed his 2" taurus .357 magnum to the crime scene tech. It was a hammerless model, small and lightweight, just right for hiding in his "maintenance man vest," as the girls often called it. Some days he carried it in an ankle holster. Now and then he left it locked in a toolbox when he was doing something on a ladder.

The tech put the gun in a clear evidence bag and sealed it. "One live round left," said West. "Let me know if you need anything else." He often wondered if any of the bankers would pick up on the concealed revolver, but no one ever seemed to notice.

The first thing he asked his boss was about carrying the piece, he told him it was his call. The security procedures were just one of the problems West found lacking. No one seemed to be the least bit observant. If you were an employee or a security guard you had the run of the place, no questions asked.

In the last 30 years the banking industry had moved away from the mostly older, all white, three piece suit, male managers and tellers, to a business that was 90% women. The majority of them were part time, a method the parent corporations often used to keep from having to pay full benefits.

The bank hired under experienced people, paid them poorly, and then wondered why their people would steal from them. Employees were routinely fired for theft and fraud, and the bank's policy was to terminate them and never follow up with charges. The employees all knew this and some took full advantage of the situation.

The manager of the Meadowgate branch, Winter Day, was hired as a teller supervisor at her previous branch. From there she transferred to Meadowgate as a teller supervisor with a slight bump in pay grade. She was only paid about $28,000 a year to work 50 or 60 hours a week and take on a ton of responsibility.

"Jack . . .?" Deverou's voice jarred him back into the moment, and back to visions of the bloody scene. "Have you been looking into the history of Day or any of the others?"

West nodded, "Yeah, she's been with the bank for about two and a half years. Meadowgate is the first branch she's worked at where she was the manager." Pulling out a file from his leather briefcase, he handed it to the agent. It had a sticker on it that said, "Monthly Maintenance Procedures." "This will tell you a little about her work history and a few interviews I did on the QT with others that knew her. She had a short but obvious fling with the manager in the North Denver branch, it ended with the manager leaving, and a nasty divorce for him."

"Go on, I'm listening," said Deverou, staring intently at the woman's security photo.

"From there, she worked at the Fairplay, Colorado branch, with similar results, and then turns up at the Colorado Springs downtown branch with a teller supervisor position."

"What happened to the Fairplay manager?" asked Deverou.

"Don't really know, he was married, now he's moved on I guess."

"So now you're going to tell me that she had an affair at this branch? I assume with the manager?"

"She did, I was here for the whole thing. His name is Bradford Taylor. They were like two little kids that couldn't keep a secret. Always touching and smiling and giggling, like no one else would notice. He was twice her age and they were always huddling together and spending a long time together in the cash room," said West. "He would send her flowers and she would play as though she had a secret admirer. He would get a single red rose on his desk once a week."

Deverou looked up from the security picture and shook his head. "I don't see the attraction; she looks kind of plain to me."

"The picture shows her in her librarian mode," said West, "with a bun and birth control glasses. Trust me, she doesn't always look that way. When she turns it on, men fall all over her. I've seen guys change places in the teller line in order to get her to wait on them. Taylor, her last manager, was the worst, she had him hooked in a couple of days. He moved on about a month ago and she got the manager's job."

Jack paused his account long enough to catch his breath and clean his glasses. "Almost immediately after she moved from the North Denver branch it was robbed by a lone gunman, and the same for the Fairplay branch."

Deverou listened intently. Do you think it was the same guy?"

"No," said West. "They appear to be unrelated, both suspects have radically different descriptions."

"What would that be?"

"One guy was tall and black and the other short and white."

A cell phone rang and both men reached in their pockets at the same time. Jack won the contest and grabbed his phone, grateful for a little diversion.

"This is Jack, who's this? Thanks, we'll be right over, ask her to wait for us. Well Bert, shall we go have a talk with the manager?"

"I'd love to. She sounds like someone I'm dying to meet."

West nodded his head silently as they ducked under the crime scene tape and headed for the hospital.

*

The hospital entrance had nearly as many police and press surrounding it as the bank. Nurses and doctors mingled with police officers and bank people. It was some kind of miracle that not one of the six other employees was injured, physically that is. No telling how these people will come out of this emotionally.

Flashing their badges, West and Deverou went through the security line and straight to the chief of ER, Dr. Jon Whitney, a casual acquaintance of West's.

"Hey doc, busy day?" asked West.

The doctor didn't see much humor in Jack's question and the look he gave him confirmed it. "If you call three dead, one wounded and half a dozen traumatized for life busy, I guess, but enough bullshit. Were you hurt?"

"Sorry, just nervous humor I guess. I'm fine, though I might fall into the traumatized class."

The three men went into a heavily secured room to see the second guard. The doctor checked the monitor and looked in his eyes. "He'll be under for tonight. You can try and get something in the morning, he's not going anywhere soon. The bullet went through his armpit and nicked some bone and cartilage, he'll recover, but he's going to hurt for a long time."

"Doctor, I'm Bert Deverou, Special Agent for the FBI, can you keep him restrained? We still don't know his part in this mess."

"No problem, he won't be leaving anytime soon."

"Bert, before we go visit the lady, let me fill you in on a few things. I've tried to be friendly with all the bankers. Most of them are women and once you gain their confidence they are pretty comfortable in confiding in you. I've worked hard to get inside. She may feel I'm still a friend, even though everyone now knows I'm bank security. That could work to our advantage."

Deverou wondered if he wasn't losing control of the crime investigation to this gray haired cowboy. He decided to go with the flow for the time being, as long as West had been so deep inside. Washington wouldn't like it if they thought he was being led down the wrong path by a bank security agent.

"Bert, put on your best stern FBI agent look and let's go meet the lady."

"I can hardly wait," said Deverou warming up to his new tough guy roll.

The two men walked to the staff lounge, where the manager was waiting, curled up in a tight ball on the far end of a long overstuffed couch. Sunken deep in the cushion, she looked impossibly small and fragile with her legs pulled up under her ankle length black dress and her head buried in a pillow. Her face was streaked with eyeliner and makeup from a steady stream of tears, but her thick black hair looked the same as it was this morning, pulled back tight and bangs in perfect position. Oversized black frame glasses covered her large dark eyes and added to her plain look.

When the two men entered the room she raised her head up and looked directly at Jack with a slight flicker of recognition, as though she was sizing up the situation.

Deverou's first look at the mystery woman seemed to confirm his first thoughts from the file photo. Plain and pleasant looking, maybe 5'- 6" and 120 lbs., definitely not your normal looking bank robbery suspect.

Winter Day set the pillow aside and stood up, the fine vertical pinstripes of her long dress showing off her thin frame and professional look, a fitting outfit for a young female banker.

As she started toward West, the tears started and she began sobbing uncontrollably. "God Jack, they're

dead. Anthony and Sandy and that poor janitor."
Throwing her arms around West, her sobbing turned
into shudders and he led her back to the couch and held
her until she began to regain her composure.

"Winter, this is Special Agent Bert Deverou. He's
handling the investigation for the FBI."

She put out her hand to Deverou, showing off her
long delicate, perfectly manicured fingers. "Hello
detective Deverou, I'm Winter Day. I'm the manager
of the Meadowgate branch."

Bert Deverou shook her hand gently, wondering
how such a slight sobbing mess as this could have
anything to do with murder and bank robbery. "Miss
Day, I know this has been a horrible time for you. But
I need to get some basic information down while the
events are still fresh in your mind."

"Can Jack sit with me while we talk?"

This took Deverou by surprise. Remembering
what West said, he pulled a chair up in front of the
couch. "Sure. The first thing I want to know is what
happened in the cash room?"

She wiped at her tears with a handful of wadded up tissue, streaking her makeup even worse. "It was just like every other day until the security guard got into the cash room. He pulled out his gun, a silver colored gun, and pointed it at my head and told me to put all the hundreds in the bag. I just did what he said." As she progressed with her story she removed her glasses and set them on the couch next to her.

Deverou could see, even with the crying and the runny makeup that she had very striking eyes. Large, wide set and coal black, she looked directly into his eyes when she talked and seemed to almost penetrate him with some unknown force.

West sat next to the young bank manager listening to the story and watching the agent write word after word. He couldn't help but wonder why he didn't just use a tape recorder.

"What happened after you filled the bag?"

"I froze up. The guard, his name is Terry, told me to get face down on the floor and not to move, he didn't have to tell me twice."

Deverou found it difficult to look away, even for a second. This woman did command attention, though he wasn't quite sure why. "Then what, did you stay in the cash room the whole time?"

"Of course, I wasn't about to go anywhere."

As the interview continued, the woman's gaze never left the FBI agent's eyes for even a moment. Her hands remained folded in her lap, not even moving to gesture as she told her story. She explained the security system and the bank's relationship with the transport company and their employees.

Deverou noted everything and was ready with a new question as soon as she finished. "Did you know the guards outside of work Miss Day?"

For a moment, West thought he noticed her tense up on the couch and just as quickly the tension went away.

"I've seen them around outside of work. I was out with friends one night and I ran into Terry and Richard. This town isn't all that big, detective Deverou."

It appeared to West that Winter Day was having her way with the FBI agent. Constantly calling him detective, instead of his real title seemed to be designed to keep him a little off guard. Her voice sounded more like a child, a 24 year old child maybe, but still a child. On the phone she sounded even younger, prompting some callers to ask for someone older, or worse, someone in charge.

Deverou decided to wrap up the interview for tonight, knowing he and this interesting young woman would be talking again. For now, he needed to get away from her unrelenting eyes.

"Miss Day . . ."

"Winter, please call me Winter, like the season. Okay detective?"

Deverou wasn't sure he wanted to know her that well, but for now he'd give her what she asked. "Okay Miss Day, Miss — Winter that is."

"Thank you detective, anything else I can do for you right now?"

"I think we're good for now, do you need a ride home?" asked Deverou.

"No, thank you, my mother is coming to pick me up."

"Okay, but I'll need to see you tomorrow. Hopefully you'll be able to answer a few more questions then. I can't imagine how you must feel after today's events."

"Detective, I'm fine. If you need anything Jack has a copy of the branch call list with all of our home phone numbers and addresses." With that, Winter Day, the childlike bank manager with the riveting eyes, stood up, slid on her shoes and disappeared down the crowded hallway."

West watched all this with amusement, knowing the agent had his hands full. "Well Bert, what do you think?"

Deverou stood up, slid the chair under the table and shook his head. "She is, hmm — unique, isn't she." Closing his notebook, he turned to Jack and motioned to follow. "I'm clocking out for now, could you use a drink?"

Jack stood up and headed for the door, "I thought you'd never ask."

Three blocks away, in a dingy strip mall bar, the two men took a seat and waited for the bartender.

Neither man talked for a few minutes, the tragedy of the day overriding all thoughts for the moment. The uncomfortable silence was broken by the gruff voice of the bartender, "Hey Jack, you there when the shooting started?"

West finally snapped out of his own thoughts. "Hi Barney, yeah, I was there, I'll tell you about it someday. This is FBI Special Agent, Bert Deverou, he's in charge of the investigation."

The bartender shoved a ham sized hand toward the agent and introduced himself. "Good to meet you agent, always happy to serve one of the good guys." The bartender brought the set up for Jack's drink to the rail and precisely mixed it, setting the bottle of gin on the back bar and placing the drink on a napkin.

"What about you Bert, what'll it be."

Deverou pulled out his pad and pen, setting it on the bar. "Coke please, and a glass of water."

"I thought you were clocked out ?"

"I just can't stop thinking about things. I guess that means I can't clock out yet."

Setting up Deverou's Coke and a large glass of water, the bartender slid West's money back to him. "This one's on me guys."

The two men raised their glasses and in unison offered a toast. "Thanks Barney," said West. As Jack watched, Deverou made more notes in his book. "Bert, I'm dying to know why you use the note book instead of a tape recorder.

"Just old school I guess, it's just the way I learned. Right now I have nine agents on the streets questioning suspects, witnesses and victims, and most of them carry a pad and a recorder. Since you and Miss Day were my only interviews the pad was more than adequate."

"So tell me Bert, be straight with me, what do you think of the lady?"

"Nearly thirty years with the Bureau and she may well prove to be one of the most interesting challenges I've ever had."

West drained his drink and motioned to Barney for another. When the drink came he tipped his glass to the agent and smiled. "She is interesting, isn't she?"

"What else can you tell me about her Jack?"

"From what I've put together, she started out life as one of two sisters of a hippie mother, each with different fathers. The mother even lived in a commune for a while, she was protesting a little of everything I guess." Finishing his drink, he motioned to the bartender again. "She was a problem teenager, doing everything she could to make people miserable, even spending a little time in a psyche ward. She was a cutter; you know what I mean, someone that cuts herself with a razor blade? She even tried to cut her wrists once."

Deverou listened to him intently making an occasional note in his book. "What else can you tell me tonight? I know it's starting to get late."
"Her IQ is 181."

That was enough to stop Deverou from writing for a moment. "Shoot Jack, I may need Sherlock Holmes on this one."

"Bert, I'm heading home. Three drinks on an empty stomach are more than my limit. Call me if you need anything or if you find the guard or the money."

"Thanks for everything Jack, can we get together at the hospital first thing in the morning."

"You got it Bert, how does eight sound?"

"Seven sounds better don't you think?"

As West stepped through the door, Deverou's pager began to vibrate, skidding erratically down the damp bar like a cheap kid's toy. He forgot he'd changed to vibrate before his interview with the manager. Looking at the Caller ID screen he recognized agent Bill Davis' number. Davis was his right hand man, a twenty year spit and polish guy, with impeccable credentials and a serious workaholic like himself. Deverou punched the talk button and started speaking instantly, "Bill, any word on the wounded guard yet?"

While he listened to Davis fill him in on his days' work, he flipped through the file folder Jack gave him earlier. When Davis finished his briefing, Bert gave him a few more instructions. "I have a couple more names for you to check out." When he finished spelling the names, he added one more instruction. "And Bill, there is absolutely nothing about their lives that I don't want to know."

By seven in the morning, the press had died down enough to find a parking place in the nearest lot. As West walked through the door he spotted Deverou immediately, talking with the Intensive Care doctor on call. He was writing in his official FBI notebook, just like yesterday. He was dressed in a dark suit with a perfect crease and a red tie, also just like yesterday. The two men exchanged morning pleasantries and headed down the hallway towards the wounded guard's room. Nodding to the two guards on either side of the door, they walked into the room.

The guard, thirty year old Richard Robbins, looked at West, and the recognition was instant. "You son of a bitch, you shot me! You freakin' shot me!"

West walked directly to the bed and looked at the guard. "You're damn right I shot you. You had your gun out and your partner was shooting, what did you expect?"

"I didn't have anything to do with it. I had no way of knowing he was planning this. I have a wife and two kids, I need the job, not this crap." Badly overweight, with an acne scarred face, and short curly hair the guard looked scared and rather pitiful.

"Richard, you've seen me around the banks before, I'm Jack West, Rampart Bank Security. This is FBI Special Agent Bert Deverou, he's in charge of this mess."

Wasting no time, Deverou got right to the point. "Tell me about your relationship with your partner outside of work. Are you buddies, do you go out together?"

The guard nodded his head and shifted uncomfortably in his bed. "We used to go out all the time. To the bar and out to the shooting range. I thought he was my friend till the last few weeks, then he turned into a jerk."

"Why the sudden change Richard?" asked Deverou.

"He wouldn't talk, no matter how much I tried to get him to," replied Robbins. "But I think it's the woman banker."

Deverou looked up from his notebook at this, "You mean Winter Day?"

"Yeah, her. The bitch in black. I think she had her hooks in him. We never went to the bar any more, never went anywhere for that matter."

West nodded in agreement, "She does wear black a lot, that's for sure."

The guard pressed his call button repeatedly, waiting for the nurse to respond. "Her black hair, black clothes and those freakin' black eyes match her heart, at least as far as I'm concerned."

Bert finished up the interview and told the guard he would be back later with more questions. The guard continued to press the call button, yelling for anyone that would listen.

West bent over the guard, "I'm sorry about the shoulder, just one of those deals."

"Screw you, thanks for nothing. Where's that freakin' nurse!"

The two men walked down the hallway and out the front door. Before they could get any farther, Deverou's phone rang. Flipping it open he began the conversation on the offensive, like always. "Bill, what have you got? Great, give me that address again, got it.

You know the procedure, button the place up, I'll be right there."

"Jack, we found the guard, he's dead. Ride with me and direct me to the 8oo block of South Weber." The address was in the older part of town, a street in the middle of the most recent urban renewal push. Most of the homes were either abandoned or in the process of being demolished. Many of the trees had been cut down and pushed to the back of the lots. When they pulled up to the address, West could see the lights of the CSPD patrol cars flashing through the piles of dead trees.

The blonde guard lay dead outside the driver's door of an old red VW hatchback with temporary plates. His vest had been removed. A large sized bullet entry wound was evident through the chest and another through his forehead. His upper left arm had a wound with a makeshift bandage wrapped around it.

Looking at the car interior, it was obvious that the guard had lost a lot of blood. The wound in the arm might not have been fatal, but the blood loss would have eventually killed him if the second shooter hadn't finished him first. The bank bag was lying inside the car, along with dozens of paper straps used to bind the bills together, and there was no sign of the cash.

The FBI crime scene investigator called to Deverou, motioning to the agent to come over to the body. West stayed with the car; he'd seen more than enough dead people lately. "Bert, I don't know if it's all that important or not, but he has a tattoo."

Just above and to the inside of the victim's left nipple was a tattoo of a single black rose. It was about three inches long, with a smooth stem and two leaves, it appeared to be very fresh.

Deverou made a few more notes in his book and climbed back into the car.

"What do you think Bert? Any idea who might have done this?"

The FBI agent looked at West and nodded his head. "I have a few thoughts . . ."

*

West and Deverou walked into the cramped command center in the bank parking lot and sat at the table. A dozen or more memos sat on the table next to a stack of files. Bert read the memos, stacked up the files neatly and wiped the table with a paper towel. Being neat was natural for him, but it became obsessive when he was working on a complicated case.

After going over a few more points with his team, they handed him another file folder. He sat it on the stack in front of him and opened it up. "Jack, my team came up with some more on Miss Day and her history with the bank. When she left the North Denver branch it was robbed two days later by the tall black man you mentioned yesterday. He got about $60,000; mostly because he knew to get both drawers at every teller station."

Deverou continued to read quickly through the file making mental notes as he went. "It looks like three days after she left the Fairplay branch it was robbed."

"By the short white guy?"

Bert nodded his head, "Looks that way, for about $35,000, at least that's what the report says."

West asked the obvious question, "Any connection between the two? Or for that matter them and her?"

"Nothing obvious that I can see here. As a teenager she was diagnosed as Bipolar. She aced her college SAT's and graduated number two in her class. Jack, you know Miss Day better than me, you want to call and invite us over to her apartment? We have a few more things to talk about."

*

The door swung open and Winter Day greeted the men with a faint smile. "Jack, detective Deverou, come in." The apartment was a standard looking rental, two bedrooms, living room and a kitchen. One couch, one chair and a small oak table nearly filled the tiny living room.

A fireplace was the focal point of one wall. On one end of the mantle was a clear bowl with a single goldfish swimming endlessly in circles, on the other end, a framed photograph of the young banker. She was dressed in a pair of bib overalls, a flannel shirt, and a blue watch cap, posed against a mountain backdrop. *Just one more incarnation of the same woman*, thought Bert.

Winter Day walked toward the back of the apartment. "Come with me, feel free to investigate anything you want, that's what you guys do, don't you, investigate things?"

The two men followed her down the hallway and turned left into the larger bedroom. A neatly made bed with a blue comforter and a television were the only furniture. A large print hung on the wall above the set. The print was a copy of a popular piece of Art Deco called *The Diner*. This particular rendition had tiny electric lights imbedded right in the picture. A wireless computer keyboard for a TV computer setup was resting on top of the TV.

As they passed by the open closet, Deverou noticed her wardrobe was almost all black, just like everyone said. Things looked to be prepared special for this event. The remarkable thing about the rooms was the stark unadorned look and the absolutely spotless, nearly sterile cleanliness. She led them by the kitchen to the living room, pulled off her shoes, and sat down on the only chair pulling her legs under her.

"What would you like to know detective?"

Deverou began to feel like a kid being led around by someone having a little fun at his own expense. She knew how to take charge of a situation.

Winter smiled up at the men, something Deverou hadn't seen until now. "You can sit if you'd like," motioning to the couch.

The men sheepishly sat down on the couch wondering when they lost control — or if they ever had control. "Miss Day — I'm sorry, Winter, can you tell me about your career with the Rampart Bank from your first position with them?"

Reaching behind her head, she released her hair letting it cascade down her shoulders. Her long wavy black hair fell well below her shoulders, framing her face and bringing to life her large black eyes. Her gaze never left Deverou's, her glasses were nowhere to be seen. She was wearing tight faded jeans, and a tight, long sleeve black tee shirt. It was tight enough to show off her shape, but modest enough to leave a little mystery. "I started at the North Denver branch about two years ago, my boyfriend and I came from Salt

Lake. We both liked Colorado so we got jobs in Denver."

"What was his name and where's he at now?" asked Deverou.

"His name is Steven Rains, we split shortly after we got there. I have no idea where he is now."

"What was your position at that branch?" asked Deverou.

"Line teller, grade 6. Two months later, I was made teller supervisor."

"Seems like a rather fast rise up the ladder. I mean as a new employee, you must have made a good impression on the manager."

"There are two reasons for that detective. First I was a much better banker than he was, check the records and you'll see I'm right. Second, I had an affair with him, he liked me."

This blunt revelation surprised Deverou, but he didn't stop writing long enough to show any reaction. "Winter, you aren't bashful are you?"

"Obviously not. Playing those kinds of games is a waste of time. I'm sure you already know that I went from there to the Fairplay branch as assistant manager. While I was there I had an affair with that manager."

"Were you a better manager than him too?"

"Of course, again, just look at the records. He was totally incompetent, even worse as a lover." Jack was visibly uncomfortable when the talk turned to her sex life, and she knew she was getting to him. Although Deverou didn't show it as much, she was getting to him too. She waited patiently for the next question, watching him fill his book with word after word.

"Winter, I assume you know that both those branches were robbed right after you left?"

"Of course detective, internal bank memos go out to all of us immediately after an incident. You seem to be preparing me for the big question, so let me skip ahead. I didn't rob any banks. I do like men and I do like sex. If those managers weren't so weak, they would still be the managers and still be married."

Feeling the need to change the subject, Deverou asked her an unrelated question. "Do you drink much Winter?"

A brief flash in her eyes showed him he scored a point, as minor as it was, he knew he had derailed her slightly.

"On occasion I might have a drink, but it's not a regular thing."

Sensing he may have found a weak spot; he pushed her a little more. "What do you like? You don't look like a beer drinker."

"I don't see how this is important detective, but I do like a gin and tonic now and then."

"Were you social friends with the men that robbed the branches?"

"No detective I wasn't"

Deverou kept up the pressure, hoping she might slip up. "Was the blonde guard, Terry, one of your lovers?"

"No detective, he wasn't. Like I just said, I didn't rob any banks. I didn't know the robbers very well and I have no connection to them."

"You didn't recruit anyone to commit the robberies for you, maybe using your obvious charms as a lure?"

Leaning slightly forward she looked directly into his eyes, and broke into a huge Julia Roberts type smile. "Why detective Deverou, you think I have obvious charms? Thank you for that, but no, as I said, I have no connection to them."

Bert felt his face begin to flush. This may be one of the toughest women he's ever known. "Winter, why do you always wear long sleeves?"

Her eyes flashed again, if only momentarily. Bert knew he scored again and waited for her response.

"You already know the answer to that detective, or you wouldn't have known to ask the question. But if you want to see my arms, just say so."

"If you could just roll up your sleeves I would appreciate it."

She stood up and pushed up her sleeves, extending her arms to the agent. Both wrists had large scars over the veins. Dozens of smaller scars went up each arm nearly to the elbow. "Happy detective? Just my version of a rebellious childhood." She stood directly in front of Deverou, nearly toe to toe, pulling down her sleeves, never moving her eyes from his.

"Is there anything else I can show you detective, anything at all?" Deverou flushed again, shook his head and stood up. When he did, he nearly knocked her over. She never moved, her black eyes staring relentlessly into his, almost daring him to say something else.

The two men thanked her for her time and walked out the door, with a strange feeling that they should be happy to get out with their lives.

*

Sitting at the table in the FBI trailer, Deverou and West went over what they learned in the last hour. West shook his head and laughed out loud, "She is something, isn't she?"

Deverou looked at the bank security agent, knowing what he had to say next would change everything. "Jack, Winter Day is a serial killer."

West stared at Deverou for a long painful minute, his face turning red, and then finally spoke. "How did you come up with that? That's pure bullshit! You think she kills people? You're way off here, not a chance!"

"Jack, listen to me. We've been on to her since the robberies in North Denver, but we couldn't make a connection to her and the bank robbers, that is until we found the body of the guard."

"What the hell does he have to do with the other robberies?"

Deverou slid a photo of the blonde guard's body in front of him. "The tattoo Jack, the black rose tattoo. We could never find the guys that did the other stickups, so it figured they skipped the country or they were dead." "When I saw the black rose tattoo I took a chance and sent out a flyer to all the Colorado counties asking if they had found any bodies with a black rose tattoo in the last couple of months. Denver found a dead guy with the same tattoo about a month ago, he's still unclaimed."

"And . . .?" said West, trying to hold back what must have been a look of disbelief.

"The Park County Sheriff's office confirms that they have a white guy in their morgue too. Same tattoo Jack. One black rose on his left breast. Want to know how they died?"

West felt like he might be sick, he felt his heart crashing through his chest and it was hard to get a full breath, "Don't tell me, one in the heart and one . . ."

His words trailed off and Deverou finished his sentence for him. "In the head Jack, she's doing business like the old Mafia guys used to do, just break the chain and there's no link to her. Head and heart."

West looked nearly overwhelmed at this wild story. "So you think she killed the guard too?"

"I do, but I don't think him killing three people in the branch was in her plan. I believe he was freelancing it. I think he just got scared and she had to take care of business after she left the hospital."

"What's next, are you arresting her?"

"No, not enough hard evidence yet, but I'm thinking of arresting you," said Deverou flatly.

West looked stunned, the thought of being arrested for murder was the farthest thing from his mind.

"What the hell are you talking about?"

"Well Jack, there are a couple of things, like the group Christmas picture of the bankers on your wall.

Miss Day had her arm around you, not any of the others."

"That's it? She had her arm around me?" "There's also the gin. The Bombay Sapphire gin you drank in your Gin and Tonic at the bar. Very expensive stuff. The bartender knew exactly what you drank from experience. Miss Day likes gin and tonic also, in fact she had a half empty bottle of the same gin along with two bottles of Tonic water on the shelf of her closet."

Deverou continued, "The guard was killed with a Ruger GP100, .357 magnum, I think there is a good chance the bullet came from his own gun. There's also the small, empty vase on your desk, the type that might hold one rose, like the old manager used to get from her."

"Where do you get this stuff, you're crazy!"
"It's all right here in my book Jack, in black and white."

West stood up on shaky legs and tried to compose himself.

"I can put this to bed once and for all Jack, if you will do one thing for me."

"What are you talking about?"

"Just take off your shirt."

Jack West turned and headed for the door, looking back at the FBI agent. "Screw you Deverou, you and the rest of your FBI buddies."

*

Standing in front of the mirror in the motel room, he looked at the new rose tattoo on his left breast. It was black with a smooth stem and two leaves. The beautiful young woman with the long black hair and the amazing black eyes stood naked in front of him. She had smooth olive skin, full hips and small perfect breasts. She also had a rose tattoo on her left breast. Her tattoo had a black flower and two leaves, but her stem was covered with thorns. On the end of each thorn was a single speck of red, a drop of blood.

Winter Day looked at West. "Do you like your tattoo Jack?"

West touched her face gently and looked into her eyes, "I love my tattoo, but I love you more, you know that."

"I know that Jack, trust me I know that. Now lay down on your back and close your eyes cowboy, I have something very special for you."

West closed his eyes and grinned while she climbed on top of him.

The .357 magnum, semi jacketed hollow point blasted through his breastbone and shredded his heart, leaving a fist sized hole in his back. The second shot exploded his skull like a rotten melon.

Winter Day, the beautiful black rose banker, put her finger in the gaping hole in his chest and pulled it out slowly. She rubbed the blood slowly around her tattoo, covering the thorns completely. Dropping the revolver on the bed she looked at the lifeless corpse. Bending down she kissed him gently, whispering in his ear, "Sorry Jack, but I'm done with you now."

The Trail

The coroner pulled back the sheet and exposed the top half of the body. The autopsy had already been performed and the death certificate issued. Cause of death: gunshot to head and chest, manner of death — murder.

The postmortem was routine police business, just a legal necessity. The manner of death was all too obvious, one large caliber bullet through the chest and one large caliber bullet through the forehead. The man who requested to view the body made a few notes in his notebook, and took several photographs. He took particular care photographing the tattoo on the left side of the man's chest.

Albuquerque's coroner looked a little closer at the unusual design. "You ever see a tattoo like that before?" he asked.

"Unfortunately, I've seen a couple of them in the last year or so," said Deverou. "You can go ahead and put him back, I have everything I need. Did forensics recover the slugs?"

"Yeah, they were .357 magnums, but there's not enough left of them for a ballistics match, probably hollow points."

The man on the table was Allan Bell, recently found dead in a cheap hotel room near old town. He was lying face up on the bed, totally naked. The crime scene photos in the folder were enlarged and very detailed. The only thing out of place was the hole in his chest and the one in his head. Both were point blank contact wounds. A blue revolver lay on the bed next to him. On his left chest was a tattoo, a black rose with a smooth stem and two leaves.

His clothes were folded neatly and hung over the chair and his shoes were slid under the bed with the socks tucked inside. A watch and ring were sitting on the dresser. It was a rather stark empty scene, thought Deverou, making more notes in his book, almost looking like it was staged for effect.

Reading through the file, it showed that Bell had been the manager at a car dealership in that part of the city. As a manager, he had taken over the business two years ago. Hiring a couple of new people in the last year had proven to be a good move, and business was better than ever.

*

The two local detectives assigned to the case sat in the office of the morgue with the FBI Agent and went over the details of the crime with him. Bert listened intently and then filled them in on what he knew about the suspect. "I've seen this crime before, once in Colorado Springs, once in Billings, and now in Albuquerque. The killer is a woman, this is her work," said Deverou, handing the detectives an enhanced photo of Winter

Day made from the one collected at the Colorado bank, and one of the tattoo.

One of the detectives asked if he had sent the two pictures out to other agencies, Deverou nodded his head, "They went out all over the country, that's how the police here and in Billings knew to contact me. I asked everyone to hang a copy of the black rose tattoo in their coroner's office. What can you tell me about the gun found at the scene?"

"It was a blue, Ruger GP100 with four live rounds left and no prints on it."

He nodded his head and noted it in his pad. Then he filled them in about his encounter with Winter Day, Jack West and the shootout at the bank in Colorado.

*

"I guarantee she's not around here any longer, she always runs after one of these deals. If you check the car dealership, I'm sure you will find that Bell was stealing from them and that he was having an affair with a pretty young woman he'd hired. More than likely she had something to do with the financial part of the business," said Bert. "The problem is, by the time we find her next victim, she's already long gone. I'm sure she's already set up shop somewhere else by now. What we really need is to know is where."

*

Rosa's Cantina, a local Mexican favorite, sat in the middle of San Antonio's famous River Walk. It had been one of the most popular nightspots in the city for nearly twenty years. The manager, a slim, pretty, dark haired woman who could easily pass for Hispanic, sat at the end of the bar shuffling through a folder of the day's paperwork. It was another busy Saturday night and like usual, the crowd spilled out onto the sidewalk and on occasion into the San Antonio River.

The young manager had started as a bookkeeper and parttime bartender about three months ago and was recently promoted to manager after the last one abruptly quit without notice. It had been a long day, and she was officially off the clock. The bartender, a thirty year old recent immigrant from Mexico named Nevada, set up a fresh drink for her and returned the gin bottle to the back bar.

Finally looking up, she gave him a small nod of thanks and turned her attention to the crowd. She had introduced some local rock bands into the mix of traditional Mexican and Mariachi music and the people were responding well to it. Several small changes she had made showed a noticeable improvement in the bottom line and the owners were more than pleased with her work.

Releasing her hair from the bun she'd been wearing; a cascade of long black hair fell down her back nearly to her waist. She was dressed in her normal long-sleeved black blouse and tiny black skirt. After unbuttoning her top three buttons she shook out her hair and finished the drink. "Nevada, be a doll and make me another please . . ."

Nevada Diaz, much taller than the usual Mexican men and considered very handsome to the women around San Antonio, mixed her another drink and then leaned over and whispered something to her.

She looked up at him and gave him a slight smile, "Maybe tonight, if you treat me right . . ."

Sitting on the bed, the woman, known as Alexa Lewis, leaned forward and looked at the day's receipts spread out in front of her. Rosa's had done over $4,800 in sales for one Saturday, the best single day since Rosa's had been in business. "So what is next Senorita Alex?" asked Diaz, sitting on the edge of the bed. He had just stepped out of the shower; his thick black hair was still wet and dripping down his chest. He had nothing on but a towel wrapped loosely around his waist.

"I think another two weeks will be about right," she said. "Then we'll have more than enough to get out of here and start over somewhere else."

"How is it you plan on getting uh, the, dinero?" Diaz had learned enough English to get by, but still reverted to Spanish when it wouldn't come to him.

"You forget, I'm also the bookkeeper, you know, el contador? The owners love me and trust me with their business."

"So lucky for me," said Diaz. "I love the senorita too . . ."

"Lucky you is right," said Alex, locking her intense dark eyes onto his. "You don't know just how afortunado you're about to be." Standing up on the bed she stripped off her clothes in a slow teasing dance. "But you'll find out for sure in two more weeks. Now drop that towel and get over here, I've got something to hold you over until then . . ."

*

Deverou sat on the bed in his hotel room. His briefcase and laptop were open and a slightly blurry photograph of a young dark haired woman looked out at him from his screen. She looked plain, with her hair pulled up in a tight bun and oversize glasses. The picture really didn't show her at her best. It had occurred to him after he met her that she was dressed this way intentionally, and she was understandably camera shy. When the woman he knew as Winter Day wanted to, she could be a remarkable beauty that commanded attention from everyone that ever crossed paths with her.

Deverou had been on her trail for nearly two years and was no closer to finding her now than when she went on the run after killing Jack West, and that was three murders ago. After all this time, he had learned more about her than he had any of his subjects before her.

She was born to a white mother and a black father. Her mother was one of the original hippies. Drugs and free love were common and she spent part of her early years in a commune. By the time she hit high school she was already smarter than everyone in the class and was a master at reading and manipulating people, including her teachers. In her Senior year she had affairs with at least two of her teachers. Her high school class photo showed a plain frizzy haired, slightly chubby girl with large glasses. The woman he met was 5'-7" and at most a hundred and twenty pounds. The class photo was even worse than the one he was using.

Deverou went over the files for the hundredth time, hoping he would find some small clue that he had overlooked before. He had convinced the director to put her on the FBI's famous "Most Wanted List," hoping he could draw a little more attention to the case. Next to her picture, he included a photograph of the black rose tattoo, maybe it would give someone the tip they needed.

In every city he worked in, he passed out flyers with the two pictures on it. He went in every tattoo parlor he could find and sent mailers out to those he couldn't get to in person, the only time he ever saw that tattoo was in the morgue. If Winter Day, the serial killer with the striking eyes was ever there, nobody had seen her, or nobody was talking.

*

It had been two weeks and Nevada Diaz was getting nervous. His fresh tattoo, a black rose, was bothering him and he wore a bandage over it every day so it wouldn't stain his shirts. Alex teased him about it, calling him her little black rose bandito.

This afternoon she was scheduled to do the banking for Rosa's and she planned to withdraw the money from the account she had attached her name to. She put the cash, almost eighty thousand in hundreds, in two large white envelopes. She also bought a pistol a few days before.

As a business manager she had no problem with the purchase, explaining how she carried large amounts of money back and forth to the bank every day. Her current identity passed the background check without any problem. The Ruger GP100 .357 magnum with the short barrel fit easily into her purse. She bought a box of hollow point bullets to go with it.

"Miss Lewis, have you ever fired a gun like this before?" asked the sales clerk. "We have a pistol range and instructors available if you need them."

"No thank you, I've used this model before, many times."

"Very good, let us know if there is anything we can do for you in the future."

"I will, thanks."

*

"Nevada, let's get out of here, I'm through with this place and ready to move on."

"Si, I am ready also," said Diaz.

After separating the cash from the night's receipts, she turned to Nevada. "Grab a fresh bottle of gin and some tonic water. Tonight will be a night to remember my handsome amigo."

"Si, a night to remember for sure!"

In a small traveler's motel west of town, Nevada Diaz checked in and paid cash for one night. Locking the door and pulling the curtains tight, he kicked off his boots and put his hat on the nightstand. Peeling off his shirt, he turned on the air-conditioning full blast. He removed the cellophane bandage over the tattoo and looked at it in the mirror. "I think the rose looks good, it's all healed up."

Alex sat at the table with a small pile of cash and a fresh gin and tonic. "Okay Senor Diaz, it's time to celebrate . . ."

Mixing himself a drink, he stripped to his shorts and lay back in the bed. "My little dark eyed devil, come here please . . ."

She put the money in her bag and looked at Diaz. "There will be no celebrating tonight unless you remove those shorts amigo . . ."

Diaz looked confused, "Shorts?" "Yes, shorts. You know, pantalones?"

"Oh, si, si — calzoncillos . . .!"

"Whatever you call them, just get them off now!"

As he removed his shorts, Alex began to slowly undress. Diaz laid back and watched this extraordinary young beauty in front of him. When he could hardly stand it any longer she climbed on top of him. Her smooth olive skin and perfect breasts captivated him. Slowly, she moved up and down rhythmically as he ran his fingers through her hair and across her breasts. Reaching up and touching her tattoo, he closed his eyes and lay his head back down, lost in the pleasure of the moment. Suddenly, he opened his eyes and looked up at her for a moment, she was staring directly into his eyes. Her black eyes were always a little unsettling to him, even now.

"Just put your head back on the pillow and close your eyes please . . ."

"Si Senorita, whatever you want."

"That's what I want. Just lay your head back in the pillow, I have a big surprise for you."

Diaz closed his eyes and nestled his head in the pillow. His life ended with the muffled sound of a gunshot. The pillow had worked well to silence it. The second shot through his forehead was equally quiet. Alexa dipped her finger in the bloody wound and rubbed it over her tattoo, as though to add a little more blood to her roses' already bloody thorns. She bent down and kissed him on the lips, "Sorry Nevada, you were much better than some, but I just don't need you anymore."

She spent nearly an hour cleaning up, dusting, organizing, and wiping down everything in the room. When she finished, it left the room looking stark and sterile and cleaner than when she came in, except for Nevada's blood soaked body. Alexa Lewis went into the bathroom and took a long shower, washing her hair to be sure there wasn't any sign of blood on her.

When she finished she got dressed in fresh jeans and a baggy sweatshirt, and put her long hair up in a bun. She put her contacts in the case and put on her heavy glasses completing the plain look she favored while looking for another place to set up shop. Nevada Diaz was lying naked on the bed, the wounds had caused massive damage, and the bed was turning red under him.

Dropping the revolver on the bed next to him, she picked up his keys, gathered her bag and the money, hung the *Do Not Disturb* sign and disappeared into the sticky Texas night.

*

In his Washington D.C. office in the FBI headquarters, Special Agent Bert Deverou finished up his report on a recent kidnapping case, and sat it squarely on the upper left corner of his desk. His secretary would file it later. On the upper right corner was a thick green folder marked Winter Day, murders. It had been over six months since the Albuquerque murder and he knew it was about time to hear from her again.

A naturally clean and organized person, when he had a tough case that was bothering him he became almost fanatical about it. His desk was shiny clean and everything on it was also clean and positioned very precisely. One of his partners once told him that his work area looked more like an operating room than an office.

Deverou knew his obsessive tendencies might appear a little over the top to some, but clearing the clutter and keeping things clean helped him focus. Outgoing went on the upper left, open cases on the upper right, and the monitor was exactly in the center of the desk. Everything had a specific place and everything was spotless.

Whenever he had a spare moment, he would open the Winter Day file and start again from scratch. As all good investigators knew, there is usually a path to your subject somewhere, you just have to find it. After several crime scenes by the same person, there's almost always some small thing that was overlooked or not understood that could possibly open the door for you.

On a pair of large white boards, he started to hang every photograph and note as well as all of the autopsy and crime scene reports. He had done this exercise many times before. After a while he would take them down and put them all back in the file. Every time he

64

put them back up it was like looking at them with fresh eyes, it was a method that had worked well for him several times in the past.

He started with the photos of the woman and the black rose tattoo side by side. Then he listed in chronological order the crimes he knew about, starting with the National Bank murders. Drawing a line to each crime scene, he ended his map in Albuquerque. He pulled out a fresh legal pad and began to make new notes for every city and he started to make lists of every fact of the cases and as many crime photos as he had from each place.

Deverou pulled his office chair in front of the boards, sat down and stared at his work. He began to list common things from the crime scene photos. With the exception of the messy killing of the armored car guard in Colorado, wherever she went, she left it super clean. The room in Billings, the one in Albuquerque and her own apartment in Colorado were all that way. *A woman after my own heart*, thought Deverou, suppressing a small smile.

After a couple of hours, Deverou removed his jacket and hung it neatly over the back of his chair. He left his office just long enough to freshen up in the restroom, splash a little water on his face and adjust his tie. Grabbing a bottle of water, he settled back into his chair and started his next list. His investigation into Winter Day in Salt Lake, her hometown, had turned up numerous pieces of information, each giving up tiny insights into her personality.

He discovered that while in college, she worked part time as a phone psychic. Another acquaintance said she tried the sex talk business for a while. She also ran a hotel housekeeping service to make money for college. Her former boss said that things had never been as clean as when she was running the crew. With such a high IQ she was basically bored during high school. What she is, thought Deverou, is the toughest adversary of my career.

According to all of his training and experience, he knew she was an unusual mix of a sociopath and a psychopath in a very young, very pretty package. Put all of this together with an exceptionally high level of intelligence and you get a very striking criminal profile that's rarely seen by most investigators.

One characteristic she had that was uncommon to most serial killers was her ability to succeed at whatever job she started. She was able to blend in like a chameleon with the people around her. Everyone that ever worked with her described her as brilliant, dedicated, efficient, charming and socially adept in any situation. Everyone that Deverou interviewed also said that she learned the business quickly and actually improved their business and the efficiency of their system.

It was as though she viewed each new place as a challenge. After she mastered the job, she got bored and took a lover, sometimes more than one. She always managed to find someone she could easily manipulate. In time she would convert the new lover into her new partner in crime. Somewhere along the way the new convert got his official membership badge to her exclusive club, a tattoo of a black rose with two leaves and a smooth stem.

Deverou started a new list. At the top he wrote: Follow-up questions. He made a column for Colorado Springs, Billings and one for Albuquerque. He started each one with Who hired her? How did she find the job? and Tattoo shops. He spent the next two hours writing down other similar questions. All of these had been asked before by him or other agents, but it was time to do it again. He would fly to Colorado Springs tomorrow and start again.

*

The view from the top of the Stratosphere Hotel was rapidly becoming one of her favorite places, particularly at night. She released her long black hair from its customary bun and let the evening breeze have it's way with it. For several months she had worked in the accounting department of the Wonderland Hotel and Casino, the newest addition in the race for the city's biggest and best resort. Always comfortable in high places, she leaned well out over the rail and looked down at the new 7,000 room glass and steel monster called the Wonderland.

The hotel's theme was definitely Las Vegas adult. Everything about it screamed adults only. The world's largest stage, the hottest shows, the biggest stars, and the most beautiful girls on the planet (as stated by the advertising on the world's largest marquee) were the standard at the Wonderland. Everything was designed for singles and couples with money, a lot of money. Rachel Roberts liked the money part; she could learn to love this place.

After four months she had been promoted to the lead position in the cashier cage on the largest of the three casinos in the Hotel. Together they routinely handled millions of dollars in cash every day. For three weeks she had been having an affair with David Falk, the department manager of all three cage operations. He was a short, doughy, balding man with a wife and two daughters who lived for his family and his Jewish faith. But he'd never had a woman like her show an interest in him before. Within a few days she had him in bed. Within a few weeks she dropped the bombshell on him, quit his casino job or she tells his wife about the affair.

After he left, she moved up to assistant cage manager under a single young, accounting school graduate. On the outside, Josh Michael was the picture of professionalism, perfectly dressed and groomed and courteous to the customers and staff alike. He oversaw the hourly accounting of all three cages and the transport of cash and chips to and from the vault, and was a very effective manager. Average height and plain looking with thinning hair and glasses, he appeared every inch the part of a number cruncher.

Roberts had already sized him up as part of her master plan, even before David quit. For a while, he was unresponsive to any of her normal manipulations. Like always, she turned on the charm that had caught so many men in her web in the past. She probed and prodded and searched for his weaknesses and within a few weeks she found it. He was an addict, specifically heroin. She had found her way into his life.

In Las Vegas a person could find anything they wanted if they had the money. In time, she quietly became his connection and his lover. Although she had used pot many times, she'd never done hard drugs before. She didn't like the idea of not being completely in control of the situation. He didn't care if she did drugs or not, as long as she filled his own needs. Once in the morning before he left, and once in the evening was his normal routine. She provided him with the small packets of powder and even helped him shoot up. She continued to make plans for her future, and they didn't include him.

*

Walking through the front door of the Colorado Springs bank, Deverou was surprised at how different it looked. The space had been gutted and completely redone. The last time he's seen the place it was a dingy old lobby full of blood and crime scene techs. He walked up to the counter and addressed the pretty young redheaded woman in front of him. "Hi Laura, I'm Special Agent Bert Deverou with the FBI," said Deverou, showing her his badge. "Can you point me to your manager please?"

"Sure, that's her, at the end of the counter, her name is Lisa."

Introducing himself, he asked if they could talk in private for a few minutes. She led him to her office and closed the door behind them. "Would you like a coffee or something else to drink Mister Deverou?"

"Please call me Bert. A bottle of water would be great, thanks."

She handed him the water and slid into her seat behind the desk. "What can I do for you?"

"I'm here reinvestigating the robbery and murders that occurred a while back, do you remember them?"

She nodded her head, "It's not really the kind of thing you can easily forget. I took over as manager after the remodel and had to restaff the branch, nobody wanted to work here right after it happened."

"Have you been with the bank a long time?"

"Twenty-one years last May."

"Did you know Winter Day, the previous manager?"

"I knew her, mostly through bank business and bank parties. We really didn't know each other socially though."

"I'm here looking for any piece of information that might help us find her, or something we might have missed before," said Deverou. "Is there anything that you can remember about her, anything that she may have said or done that stands out in your memory?"

"All I can really remember about her is that late one night, after a company party where we both had a few drinks, she asked me if I thought she was attractive."

"What did you say to that?"

"Well, I saw men line up at her window just to get a chance to talk to her. I always thought she was kind of plain looking myself, but men obviously saw something in her that I didn't. But I told her yes, I didn't want to hurt her feelings. I heard later that she had asked a few other women the same question too." Deverou asked a few more questions, thanked the manager and moved on to his next interview, Bradford Taylor, the manager that Winter Day had the affair with.

Taylor had arranged to meet him at the restaurant next door. Taking a booth in the back of the room, Deverou showed his credentials and filled him in on why he was here. This was their first meeting, one of his other agents did the original interview. "I appreciate you taking the time to talk with me Mister Taylor."

"No problem, though I'm surprised you haven't caught up with her by now, it's been almost two years."

Deverou hated to be reminded how long this case had been going on, he really hoped to get some fresh information to move it along. "I'm surprised too, but we never give up, we will get her. I need to ask you some questions about your relationship with her and why you broke up."

"Sure," said Bradford, shrugging his shoulders and taking a long pull from his beer. "She cost me my marriage and my job with the bank, so I don't have any reason to hold anything back."

"Did you hire her as your assistant at the Meadowgate Branch?"

"Sadly yes, I was the one responsible for bringing her to this branch, something I'll have to live with forever."

"How long after she got there did you become lovers?"

"Right to the point huh? I'd say about three weeks after she arrived she had me hooked. She had an apartment that she shared with her mother. Conveniently mom was gone and she asked me to come over and help move some furniture." Taylor finished off the beer and ordered another. Deverou could see that even after all this time he was uncomfortable bringing up this old history. "We were in bed inside of ten minutes."

"How was she as a banker, Bradford? Did you trust her?"

"She was far and away the best worker and the sharpest mind I've ever seen in the business. She never made mistakes, everything always balanced and I eventually trusted her with everything. She ran the day-to-day bank business and I ran the commercial banking and loan dept."

"Tell me about when you quit the bank."

"I didn't really choose to quit, she blackmailed me, told me if I didn't leave the Rampart Bank system immediately, she would go to my wife and tell her everything. She said she didn't want to hurt my family, she just wanted me gone, can you believe that?"

"Mister Taylor, I can believe just about anything with this woman. Is there anything else that you can tell me about her that might help me find her, anything at all? Even if it seems really insignificant?"

Taylor finished his beer and motioned to the waitress for another one. "She was an absolute cleaning freak, generally wore black outfits, always long sleeves to cover her scars and had the wildest, most intense black eyes I've ever seen, she also had a couple of odd tattoos."

Deverou already knew most of this information but interrupted him when he mentioned tattoos.

"Tattoos? She had more than one tattoo?"

"Yeah, she had this strange black rose above her left breast and a black widow spider on her left wrist. She always kept it covered by her watch."

"Anything else?"

"She drank only Bombay Sapphire Gin and tonics and was a vegetarian. Oh, there's that cleaning smell too. That's about all I guess, except you probably don't want to hear this but she was one hell of a lot of fun in the sack . . ."

Deverou ignored the comment about her sexual prowess, "What about the cleaning smell?"

"It's probably nothing," said Taylor, "but after she did her general cleaning she wiped things down with some sort of disinfectant, it had an unusual smell, kind of like cantaloupe but very mild. I smelled it every time I was in her house or car. She used it at her bank work station too."

"Did you get to know her mother?"

"That's another mystery, she said she shared her apartment with her mother, but I never met her. I never saw so much as a single photo of her."

Deverou closed his notebook, thanked Taylor for his time and handed him his business card. "If there's anything at all that you remember later, please call me right away."

"I will," said Taylor. "Agent Deverou, please let me know when you get her."

*

The casino was more crowded than usual for a weeknight, and a guest had just won a large jackpot on a progressive slot machine. Rachel Roberts and one of the floor managers walked over to the winner to verify the jackpot and arrange for payoff. After so many years of living in the shadows of life, she found herself enjoying the constant action of Las Vegas and the casino more than she ever thought she would. She also knew it was a dangerous place for her to work. As much as she liked it here, there was always the chance someone might recognize her.

She had done her homework well, and the first part of her plan was working smoothly. After forcing her manager out, she was able to move up to a position that gave her better access to the money and find the perfect mark for her partner. As long as he could stay high, he was happy with their arrangement. She gave him sex and kept him in drugs, and he would do anything to keep them coming. In this case, anything would mean robbing the Wonderland Casino.

Stealing from the Wonderland was proving to be more of a challenge than anything she had ever tried before. Compared to a Las Vegas casino, robbing the bank was child's play. After six weeks of working the cage with Josh, she saw a possible flaw in the security when they transferred the cash from the cage to the counting room in the main vault. After running through the details for several days she decided they would be ready to do it in about two weeks.

Her roommate thought she was a perfect example of someone with a compulsive, over the top cleaning disorder. Spotless to the level of a hospital operating room, not a single book or coaster was out of place. Even the TV remote was clean and neatly placed in a small basket in the center of the coffee table. The whole apartment was filled with some kind of faint odor from the disinfectant she used almost every day, something he never really got used to.

Rachel sat back on the couch with her legs tucked under her while she read a book. Josh had turned on the television and was watching the local news when his nighttime fix began to flood his system. Laying his head on the arm of the couch, he closed his eyes and let the drug take over.

Rachel reached for the remote to shut off the program when she suddenly froze and stared at the set in shock. It was a special segment the local station was broadcasting. They took a two minute segment from the America's Most Wanted show and replayed it every Friday night for the viewers in their area.

Rachel stared at the screen in disbelief, she was looking at a slightly blurry photo of herself and one of a black rose tattoo. The narrator said her name was Winter Day. She was wanted for bank robbery and murder and told the story of her victims and the tattoo. The speaker asked for all tattoo artists to look at the photo and please call them if they had ever seen it before. Information on the screen said to call FBI Special Agent Bert Deverou at the FBI's Most Wanted hotline and gave the number in large text.

Rachel Roberts, AKA Winter Day, clicked off the set and looked at Josh. He was sleeping and hadn't seen the report. It had been nearly two years since she had thought about Bert Deverou and Colorado Springs.

She would have to act quickly if her plan stood a chance to work. Both didn't have to work until the Monday night shift. Fortunately, she had everything she needed, including her gun. In the morning she would lay out the plan in detail to him.

*

Deverou had decided to rent a car in Colorado. He was going to make a circuit of Colorado, Montana, Utah and New Mexico. He was more determined than ever to catch up to Winter Day, the Black Rose Banker, as the television report called her. He had reinterviewed everyone that he could find in Colorado Springs, Fairplay and Denver, and was now driving towards Billings Montana. She had become the obsession in his life, the only thing that mattered to him. Deverou had been divorced for years, a marriage claimed by too many days on the road for the bureau and not enough with his family.

After three days in Billings, he had uncovered very little that he didn't already know. This time, she found a job as an accountant for a local sports arena under the name of Katie Dunn. It was a busy place, promoting everything from a local semipro hockey team, to rodeos, concerts and civic gatherings of all types. She was hired by a young go getter named, Bruce Compton, who wore ostrich boots, a silver rodeo buckle and an enormous Stetson. He had proven to be an easy conquest. Single, nerdy and very arrogant, he hit on her the first day on the job.

The office people Deverou interviewed all said that it was obvious to everyone that they were having a relationship and that she had him in her web within a week. After two months she was promoted to assistant manager over several longtime employees and worked directly for him.

Two months after her promotion, Compton was found dead in a motel room with a black rose tattoo on his chest and two bullet holes in him. At the arena, Katie Dunn and nearly ninety thousand dollars of gate receipts were also missing.

When Deverou was ready to leave Billings, he had learned that everyone remembered the affair with Compton, she was well respected as an accountant and well liked as a coworker. One employee told him that she was definitely brilliant when it came to numbers, she had bailed other employee's out of trouble more than once. Two women also remember that she had asked them if they thought she was attractive.

Deverou left Montana and headed for her home town, Salt Lake City. He'd already sent every bit of information he could find about his subject to the bureau's profile team and they didn't come up with much more than he already had. Reading their report in his hotel room the next night just frustrated him more than anything. They noted that she had a problem with self-esteem. Her overachieving in the workplace was an attempt to make up for her lack of self-esteem when it came to her appearance. She was always aware that she was the smartest person in the room, but she constantly needed someone to tell her that she was beautiful. That's where the need for a lover came in. Once she secured him, she had him get the tattoo as proof she had the whole package. "Goddamnit . . ." said Deverou out loud, throwing the file across the bed. "I know all that already . . ."

He knew the problem came when that giant brain of hers started to get bored, and it didn't take long after the affair when it started to reach that point. When she'd finally had enough of the current situation, she would begin to look for a way out. After she made the decision to leave, she had to lose the lover and get some traveling money. "Well, Miss Winter Day, I have a big brain too," said Deverou out loud, "and I won't get bored looking for you, you can count on that."

In Salt Lake, Deverou drove to the hospital and stepped off the elevator at the sixth floor. The sign said Muller Psychiatric Unit. At the counter he identified himself and asked for Doctor Hamilton. The nurse looked up at him. "Do you have an appointment?"

"Yes, it's for ten AM," said Deverou.

When Deverou walked into the office, an older, bearded man stood up and offered his hand. "I'm Doctor Hamilton, good to meet you."

"Thanks for taking the time to talk with me doctor, you know that I'm here about Winter Day?"

"Yes, my assistant filled me in. Agent Deverou, when it comes to information on patients, you know what the standard answer is, right?"

"I do doctor, but let me fill you in on what's she's been up to since you last saw her, if you don't mind."

"Go ahead, I'm listening."

"Winter Day is responsible for at least four murders that we know of, if not more, as well as at least three bank robberies. She's now on the FBI's most wanted list, only the ninth woman ever to make the list."

Deverou outlined the basic case against her and the fact that she's still out there operating somewhere in the United States as we speak. "I'm here hoping that maybe you could give me something that can help me catch up to her before she kills anyone else."

Opening the file in front of him, he began to look through it. "Give me a moment to refresh my memory please."

"Go right ahead."

"Ok Agent Deverou. What you tell me is terrible, no doubt. But I have to tread lightly here, no recording of this conversation, I'm sure you understand . . ."

Deverou nodded. "Fair enough doctor, but please keep in mind that she has no reason to stop killing unless I can catch her."

Hamilton stared at the file a little longer. "I remember her very well. She was one of my most challenging patients. The fact is, when the woman sitting across from you is smarter than anyone you've ever met, I knew there would be some interesting sessions."

"Doctor, did you see anything in her that you thought might lead to this kind of violence?"

"I can't say that I saw anything in her that would predict a serial killer, but when you have a recorded IQ of 181, it's really easy to manipulate people. Those in my profession are always looking for clues to trying to formulate a diagnosis, she knows that very well, and can lead the therapist wherever she wants. I would imagine it's not unlike some of the people you deal with."

"What about her home life? I know a little about it, but did she suffer any particular kind of abuse?"

"My case files say there wasn't, but again, she only tells you exactly what she wants you to know," said Hamilton. "I always thought she was covering up something about her past, but with her you never really knew. She could convince anyone of anything she wanted to. One trait of the sociopath is the ability to stare into someone's eyes seemingly forever without blinking. If you ever talked to her you'd understand, she has remarkable black eyes that can sometimes frighten people."

Deverou couldn't forget her intense stares, the doctor was right about that, they really could frighten someone. "How old was she when she was brought here?"

"Just sixteen," said Hamilton. "She'd been hurting herself and attempted suicide more than once, she has the scars to show for it too."

"I remember. I saw them once in Colorado Springs when I questioned her about the robbery. It looks like she always wears long sleeves these days."

"I'm not surprised, like a lot of people, she has terribly low self-esteem. She knows she's the smartest person in the room, but has always considered herself unattractive. I think the scars add to her dislike of her appearance."

"How long was she here?"

"Two different times, ages sixteen and eighteen, for a total of about six months."

"What about medications, did you prescribe something for her?"

"Yes, we tried several things. Her biggest single issue was a serious bipolar problem. I prescribed various antidepressants and lithium carbonate, but she only took them when she wanted," said Hamilton, handing Deverou a list of what she had taken. "She was the only person I ever treated that was truly smart enough to know when she was in a bad bipolar swing, and would take it if she felt she needed it, very few people can manage themselves like that."

"Doctor Hamilton, can I call you if I come up with more questions?"

"No problem, just remember our no recording agreement."

After a few more questions Deverou wrapped it up and thanked the doctor. Finishing up a few more interviews in Salt Lake, he went back to the hotel, organized his notes and called the office. He asked them to research any disinfectants with a faint odor of cantaloupe or some kind of melon. He'd like to know the brand and where it was available. The next morning he was up early headed for Albuquerque.

*

Rachel Roberts counted the cashbox for the second time that night. The total was slightly under two hundred thousand dollars, not unusual after a four hour weekday shift. Company policy dictated that no more than four hours can pass before the excess is taken to the vault, or no more than two hundred and fifty thousand dollars can be held in the excess cashbox at any given time.

When one of the limits was reached, the person in charge of the cage counted it, locked the two locks on the box and called for a security team to transport the cash to the vault. When it came time to transport, the cage supervisor accompanied two guards and the money cart into the outer vault room. This was as far as a cage employee could go. When they were all inside, the guards and the cage supervisor signed the transfer log, and the money became the responsibility of the vault. After the cage supervisor left the outer room, the outer door was closed and the cart was rolled into the inner vault, a place few people ever get to see.

Roberts had become friendly with most of the security staff at the hotel. She had found what she believed to be a weakness in the system, and it didn't take long for her to confirm it. At Crazy Bob's, a small casino and bar used mostly by low end local gamblers, she met a couple of the vault guards and began to work them for information. Usually about three beers and a little flirting would get her whatever she wanted.

She learned that the carts were rolled into the outer vault, signed off, and after the cage supervisor left the room, moved into the main vault. The problem, according to the security guys, was that the people from the inner vault were supposed to take the cart inside immediately. In reality, they were so busy and understaffed that sometimes the carts sat in the outer vault for as much as half an hour, even forty five minutes on really busy days.

She built her plan from there; the first thing was to get her and Josh's schedule set up the way she needed it. The second thing was to do it when they were busy. A busy day meant more money in the cage and a longer delay at the inner vault. Roberts was nervous. This was something out of her usual routine. It was also a lot more cash than she had ever taken before.

"Josh, how do you like your tattoo?" asked Rachel.

"Well, it's kind of cool, but why don't you want me to show it to other people?"

"Because, it's our special thing, just between us." Josh looked at the black rose in the mirror for a long moment. "As long as you come with the deal."

Standing next to him, she pulled her t-shirt over her head, and stood naked staring at Josh. "Now strip down lover and you'll find out exactly what comes with this deal . . ."

*

When Deverou got to the Albuquerque police station, the detective had the case file waiting for him. After an hour of sorting through it and comparing it with his FBI case file, he was ready to give it up when he saw a small clear evidence bag with a piece of torn paper inside. It had been stuck to the side of the box.

"Do you know what this is?" asked Deverou.

The detective looked at it for a moment. "Not really. It was stuck to the side of the wastebasket in the hotel room. We don't know what it's from, but it was probably just unrelated trash."

Bert stared at the paper for a few seconds, "I need to take this, can I sign it out?"

"Sure, but I don't think it means anything as far as the case goes."

Deverou left the station and headed to the nearest tattoo shop he could find. Walking in the door of the small shop he identified himself to the owner and showed her the piece of paper. "Can you tell me what this is?"

She looked at it for a moment, "Yeah, it's tracing paper. It's what we use to put the design onto the skin before we start with the actual tattooing procedure."

"You're positive about that?"

"Of course I'm positive, we use it all the time. You can see a small, curved black line right along the torn edge, it's part of the design." Returning to his hotel room, he dialed Doctor Hamilton in Salt Lake.

"Hello Agent Deverou, questions already?"

"Just one doctor. Do you know if Winter Day had any skills as an artist? Like drawing or painting?"

"I have a few of the notes she made while in the office, they look more like the scribbles of a bored person than art, at least to me."

"Do they show any skill?"

"I'd say so, but they're mostly flowers. Some kind of abstract looking roses I think."

"Thanks doctor, I appreciate your help." "That's all you need?" asked Hamilton.

"That's all for now, you've been a great help, thanks again."

*

Deverou pulled a pint bottle of whisky from his briefcase and poured it over a hotel glass full of ice. In his long career, this was the first time he'd ever had a drink while working on a case. This one was different, and it was beginning to wear on him. It was already the longest case he had ever worked, and Winter Day was the most complex criminal he'd ever run across.

After downing the second whisky, he laid back on the bed and stared at her picture. "You are something special Miss Winter Day," said Deverou out loud. "Hundreds of agency man hours have been spent looking for a tattoo artist that did the black rose on your victims, and you're doing it yourself!" Bert Deverou closed his eyes. "But, I will find you my Black Rose Banker, trust me, I will find you . . ."

*

Rachel knew she had to act quickly if they had a chance to make her plan work. Now that she was on the FBI's most wanted list, her picture was out there. She was risking someone at the casino would recognize her.

The groundwork for the plan had already been done, and everything was in place to do it on second shift tonight. She had two matching canvas bags with a large sunflower design, big enough to hold plenty of cash. One she had been carrying to and from work for weeks and the second one neatly folded inside the first. "Mister Michael, it's almost time to send the cart in."

"Let's go ahead and audit the cart Miss Roberts," said Josh, knowing that security was watching and listening to everything they said.

Moving the cart into the back room of the cashier's cage, they started the audit procedure. Thanks to her flirting and drinking with the security guys, they had already discovered a way to position themselves to block the view of the cameras. They had told her that there are always a few blind spots that couldn't be found, most of them very small. Security would never admit to it, but they are there. She had found a way for her and Josh to block them, but it had to happen very quickly before anyone watching got suspicious.

Unlocking the cart, they removed all the currency and ran it through the counting machines making the necessary entries in the log in full view of the camera like always. Stepping momentarily in front of the cameras, Roberts pulled the extra bag from under her blouse and Josh put all the large bills quickly inside. It took less than twenty seconds to get the cash, relock the cart and walk to the front of the cage.

"I'm going for my break Mister Michael, I'll be back in fifteen minutes," said Roberts.

Josh Michael acknowledged her with a nod and called for vault security. Roberts walked out of the cage with her bag over her arm, across the casino floor and through the front doors.

*

Deverou grabbed the phone and the aspirin at the same time. It was his boss in Washington. "Bert, she hit again, this time in San Antonio. You need to head there right away, the local agent, Bob Pierce is waiting for you."

Deverou, struggling to focus through the hangover rubbed his eyes.

"Bert, Bert — are you there?"

"Yessir I'm here, Winter Day has killed again? In San Antonio, is that right?"

"We're sending all the details right now, get on a plane right away, they need you."

"I'm on my way to the airport right now." After dropping his rental car at the airport, he chartered a flight to San Antonio, Agent Pierce met him at the gate and they were at Rosa's Cantina on the river walk twenty minutes later.

Bert looked at the Rosa's Cantina sign for a moment before he went in. "Just like in the song, huh?"

Pierce nodded. "Just like in the song, except the cowboy wasn't the one that died, the bartender did." The restaurant was back to normal, but Pierce knew that Bert would want to interview the owners and employees. After the interviews they went to Pierce's office and started in on the case files. "This happened a couple of months ago Bob, why did it take so long to get on it?" asked Deverou.

"Local Police have been working on it for months. When they couldn't get anywhere, they called us. I don't think they wanted us involved, but the families were putting a lot of pressure on them. Washington realized right away from the M.O. that it was probably your bank robber so we jumped in."

"It's her for sure, but since it took so long for us to get the call, I guarantee she's already working some other sucker right now."

"What else do you want to see?"

"The coroner that did the autopsy on the victim," said Deverou.

Walking into the Bexar County Coroner's office, Deverou asked for Dr. Tyler, the pathologist that did the autopsy on Nevada Diaz. "He had massive wounds in his head and chest from a large caliber firearm, Agent Deverou. They found the pistol next to him on the bed."

"Did he have a tattoo Doctor?"

"Yes, some kind of black flower, a rose I think," said Tyler, handing him a photo.

"Doctor, do you have a bulletin board around here?" asked Deverou. "Someplace that you might put up information on cases from the FBI?"

"Right over there," said Tyler, pointing at a long board filled with paperwork and memos of all kinds.

Deverou walked up to the board and leafed through its thick layer of notices. Pulling out a long buried sheet of paper titled FBI Notice: Looking for Black Rose Tattoo. Below the title was a photo of the same rose tattoo he just saw in the old coroner's file.

"Son of a bitch!" Deverou wadded up the flyer and bounced it across the room in frustration. "Thanks for nothing doc, we could have been on this the day you did the work! All you had to do was look on your own goddamn bulletin board!" Deverou stormed out of the room leaving Pierce standing with the red faced doctor.

*

"Goddamn incompetent assholes," said Deverou, downing another whisky.

"I understand Bert," said Pierce. "It's frustrating for sure, but you know you'll get her sooner or later."

Ordering one more round, Deverou filled him in on his history with Winter Day, and what kind of a trail she leaves. "The problem is, I can't get ahead of her because there's no way of knowing where she'll turn up next."

Pierce finished his drink and prepared to head home for the night. "Where do you suppose she goes between her crimes? Maybe she goes somewhere special to spend her money?"

*

Deverou sat in the hotel room mindlessly watching the television news. He began to make a few notes in his book. The first thing he wrote was, where does she go between killings? He stopped right there. That might be the key to tracking her down. He called Washington and left a detailed message, "I need everything there is on where Winter Day came from and where her family came from. Dig deeper, do we have a DNA sample from her? I want everything there is to know about her and her linage."

The Capture

For the second time in as many days, Deverou was startled awake by his phone. "This is Deverou," he said, sitting up in bed looking for the aspirin.

"Agent Deverou, this is Mike Banks, in forensics. You requested a DNA search on your subject Winter Day?"

"Yeah, I did, tell me you have good news."

"I might have something you can use, but it's just a possible starting point."

"I'll take anything you have, anything."

"There were a few unknown hairs from the Colorado bank robbery in the material we have here. It appears that they were collected from the body of one of the suspects that was killed off site," said Banks.

"They'd never been tested for anything before, so I took a close look at them."

"Don't leave me in suspense any longer, what did you find?"

"I found four undyed black hairs, two broken short and two very long ones. Two of the four still had the tag on it. After full DNA and genetic testing we have a great profile on the provider of the samples. I'm sending you the report right now."

"Can you give me a nutshell version while they're on the way?"

"Sure, but remember we don't have anything from your subject to compare it to, I can't really say it's positively her."

"It's her, what else?"

"The genetic testing indicates that the subject has Polynesian and Asian bloodlines, as well as Negro and Caucasian, the details are in the report."

"That's great Mike, thanks a lot for getting right on this."

Deverou lay back in bed and waited for his printer to spit out the report. Polynesian and Asian bloodline, thought Deverou. I can only think of one place in the states where that might be very common. Skimming over the report in the hotel restaurant he made a couple of notes and finished his breakfast.

Looking at his watch he calculated the time difference between San Antonio and Honolulu, then called the agent in charge of the Hawaii bureau.

"This is Agent Jordan Travers of the FBI, what can I do for you?"

Deverou introduced himself and gave him a crash course on his case and about the new DNA evidence.

"Jordan, if I remember my history class very well, I seem to recall that Hawaii is home to a lot of old line Polynesian families, and a lot of them also have Asian roots. I'm probably just grasping at straws here, but I need to start looking at some different angles if I'm going to catch up to her."

"You're right about the islands' history and it doesn't sound like a bad place to look. What can I do for you right now?"

"How about meeting me at the airport and giving me a little tour?"

"You're coming out?"

"I think that would be best. I'll send you all the case information and the flight information. I really feel I need to get on the ground and spend some time there. I'm sure the hell not getting anywhere hanging around here."

"Okay Bert, I'll meet you at the airport and get together some information on the Asian and Polynesian communities for you."

"Thanks Jordan, I've been looking forward to a change of scenery. I'll see you then."

*

Deverou walked into the concourse and saw Travers waiting near the ticket desk. After introductions they headed for the nearest restaurant. "Sorry Jordan, I never get enough sleep or enough food on those long flights, I need a quick burger to keep me upright."

"No problem, it'll give us a chance to go over the case."

After wolfing down the meal, he ordered more coffee and opened the case files. "You read the material I sent you?" asked Deverou.

"Yes, twice, she looks like a pretty interesting case. Are you thinking she has connections here?"

"The bureau's forensic guys did complete DNA and ancestry testing and she definitely has roots in both Asian and Polynesian bloodlines, as well as a white mother and a black father. She has black hair, very dark eyes and olive colored skin. She's kind of an exotic looking woman."

"I imagine she would be unique with all those different roots," said Travers.

"Truth is, I have no idea where she's from or where she is right now, but I'm out of ideas. I thought if I could learn something about the Asian and Polynesian communities here, I might start showing her picture and the FBI wanted poster around and see if I get any hits. I believe she's working somewhere in the mainland right now. I wouldn't be surprised to get a call any time saying she's killed again."

"I brought you a book on the history of the different ethnic bloodlines in Hawaii, and a couple of maps that show the heaviest population areas of each one marked out on them," said Travers, handing him a thick folder.

"You have a pretty daunting job ahead of you."

"Yeah, I know, but like I said, I have to start somewhere. Is there any chance that you might have an agent that you can spare for a while? Maybe someone that knows these communities pretty good?"

"Normally I'd have to say no to that request, but since this is one from the most wanted list I'll make it happen. If you want to get settled into your hotel and get your rental car, I'll meet you at the office in the morning. We can set up a place for you to work."

It was still early, and Deverou went out and sat by the pool. From here he was only a couple hundred yards from the beach. After spending most of his working life in D.C. he had to admit that this was a pretty good gig. Nobody ever gave up these jobs unless they retired or died.

When the waitress came by he looked at his watch for a moment. *What the hell, it's close enough*, said Deverou to himself. "Double bourbon and water please, hold on, make that a double gin and tonic, I need to try one of those."

After four doubles, Deverou returned to his room and thought about ordering some food. He finally woke up at 8:45 to the sound of his phone ringing and a thunderous headache.

"This is Deverou."

"Bert, this is Jordan, are you coming in?"

With his head crashing and the room spinning, he gave a mumbled answer. "I apologize Jordan. I guess the jet lag got to me. Let me take a shower and I'll be right there." He threw down several aspirin and took a long shower hoping it would help his hangover. He drove from the hotel to the nearest fast-food place he could find and ordered coffee. "Hot, black and strong, the largest one I can get," he said to the voice from the speaker.

"Would you like a breakfast sandwich with that sir?"

"Just coffee."

*

The FBI's Honolulu office was a striking glass and steel building with large offices on the fourth floor and great views in every direction. Travers led him to an empty conference room. Every file had been set out neatly and he had a computer, a printer and a stack of maps of the islands ready for him.

Travers brought another agent into the room and introduced him. "Bert, this is Agent Kai Franklin, he's a Polynesian-Hawaiian native and a walking reference book on the history of the islands." Deverou stuck out his hand and it was immediately swallowed up by the huge paw of an enormous brown skinned man at least six-foot-six and three-hundred pounds. As large as he was, his abdomen was flat and his biceps bulged noticeably under his shirt. "Bert, good to meet you. The boss says you want to learn something about the Polynesian people of the island?"

"Yeah. I have a serial killer that has operated for at least several years without much interruption. We were lucky to be able to get a full DNA analysis on her. We didn't get a hit in the system but the testing shows that her ancestry has Polynesian and Asian DNA. Since I haven't been able to catch up to her for the last two years, I thought I might look into her genetic background. The only place in the country that I can think of that may have a large concentration of that particular ethnic mix would be here. It's just a wild guess at the moment, but at least it's something for me to look into."

Franklin nodded his head. "We do have a large population of Polynesians with Asian roots; I'm included in that group too. I've been through the files you sent and it's not impossible she could have some family around here. I have to say though, the photo's you sent weren't really all that great, it's hard to tell exactly what she looks like."

"You're right, they aren't great, but it's all I have at the moment."

"This tattoo of the black rose, that's common on all of her victim's?"

"Every one of them has it on their left chest. I think she did them herself, like she's marking her territory or something."

"I'll run the case information through the local departments and see if we get any matches," said Franklin.

"That's a good idea but I have this strange feeling she goes somewhere between her killings and relaxes or spends her money," said Deverou. "Wherever that is, I would be willing to guess she's pretty low profile and doesn't have a criminal past."

"I almost hope she is here, just so I can meet her in person, not to mention the chance to take down one of the bureaus' most wanted suspects and a female serial killer at that."

*

Franklin pulled out of the parking garage and headed for downtown Honolulu. "There's a small downtown museum I want to show you, it's got a good display on the ethnic roots of Hawaii. It's run by my aunt Kalani. She's a retired history teacher and the smartest person in the world."

"Really, the smartest person in the whole world?"

"That's what me, my sisters and brothers thought when we were little kids," said Franklin. "We thought she knew everything there was to know, so she must have been the smartest person in the world."

"I can hardly wait to meet her Kai, but she might not want to waste her time with someone as slow to catch on as me," said Deverou with a smile.

"No problem, she'll be happy to work with you, but we have to bribe her first."

"Bribe her? What do we bribe her with?" asked Deverou, playing along.

"Hawaiian sweet rolls. They're a local favorite here, kind of a sweet tasting dinner roll. A lot of people put jam or honey on them. She won't buy them for herself because she's afraid she'll get addicted to them and get fat. "You'll appreciate that more when you meet her."

"Sounds good to me. Now that you mention food, I could use some breakfast first."

After breakfast and several more cups of coffee Deverou was ready to go meet the smartest person in the world for a history lesson. The museum was small but packed with displays and artifacts of all kinds. From somewhere in the back of the room a booming voice hollered "Kai, my little baby keiki! Where are my sweet rolls.?"

"My sweet 'anakie, I have them right here, come out and hug me!"

A few seconds later a short, middle aged Hawaiian woman rushed towards Kai and threw her arms around him. Deverou understood Franklin's comment about her not wanting to get fat. *She must be nearly 300 pounds, if she's a pound,* thought Bert.

"And just who is this haole you brought to me? Some kind of a tourist?"

"What's a haole," asked Deverou, looking up at Kai.

"It means foreigner, she's just giving you a hard time, she does it to everyone."

Franklin filled in his aunt on why they were there and asked if she had time to talk with them. "For my baby keiki I always have time, but this haole may be unteachable, it may cost him extra sweet rolls . . ."

"You teach him and I'll keep you in sweet rolls 'anakie, I promise."

"Kai, what does 'anakie mean?"

"In Hawaiian it means aunt or maybe auntie, keiki means nephew. She really does know more about these islands than anyone I've ever known. If your killer has family roots here, she would be the one to help you find them."

"I'm ready if she is," said Deverou. "Just one thing Bert . . ."

"What's that?"

Franklin broke out in a huge grin. "Don't let her run out of sweet rolls . . ."

*

The small motel sat back from highway fifteen, just outside of Mesquite Nevada. You almost had to know where it was when you were driving, or you would miss it. She'd chosen the spot to meet up with Josh after the robbery of the Wonderland. He was already there when she arrived. Inside the room she found Josh lying on the bed, he'd just shot up and was watching the television news.

"Anything on the news about the casino," asked Roberts, as she dropped her bag alongside the bed.

Michaels shook his head. "Nothing so far, but the hotels prefer not to broadcast these things if they don't have to. I doubt anyone will ever hear about it."

"Good, I'm going to take a shower, then we can celebrate, want to join me?"

"I'll get some ice to chill this bottle of champaign first. I bought it special for tonight, then I'll be right in." When Josh walked into the bathroom, the curtain was open and Rachel was completely lathered up. Her long hair covered her left breast and the soapy water ran down and around her right breast, sliding slowly around her nipple and disappearing into the foam at her waist.

Josh quickly stripped and stepped in. "My God, what did I do to deserve such a beautiful woman?" "I guess it's just your lucky day Mr. Michaels. Now kiss me before I change my mind."

Running his hands down her back, he pulled her close, kissed her deeply and held it for a long moment. After several minutes of exploring her body in intimate detail, they moved to the bed and continued their lovemaking, with Rachel mounting him and bending over, sliding her breasts across his lips.

She reached down and picked up her bag and sat it next to them on the bed. Reaching inside with one hand she pulled out a stack of money and showed it to Josh. "What do you think lover, did I do good?"

Josh looked at the large stack of hundred dollar bills and grinned, "I'm having sex with the hottest woman in the world, and she's showering me with hundred dollar bills — it really is my lucky day."

Rachel was beginning to move faster and faster and told him to close his eyes and just enjoy what was to come. She could sense Josh getting close to the end, and reached for a pillow with one hand and into her bag with the other. Placing the pillow gently across his chest, she waited for his climax. When he reached the final seconds she pulled the revolver out of her bag.

The sound was muffled by the pillow like she knew it would be. She moved the pillow and the gun to his forehead and fired again. Bending down and kissing him, she looked into his dead eyes, "Thanks for your help." Dipping her finger into his blood, she rubbed it across her tattoo. "Goodbye Josh."

Roberts dropped the gun on the bed, poured herself a glass of champaign and began the process of cleaning up. Pulling out a plastic trash bag, she put in everything she didn't want to leave behind, including both their cell phones and his wallet then tied it shut.

Still naked, she walked through the room carefully checking every inch of the scene making sure there wasn't the slightest bit of evidence anywhere. Then she cleaned off the gun and laid it next to Joshes' lifeless body. She left all his clothes neatly folded on the nightstand and his shoes tucked under the bed. She placed his heroin kit on the table alongside of the clothes.

After another shower she poured a second glass of champaign and finished dressing. When she was done she pulled a bottle of disinfectant from her bag and used it on her hands. Slipping on a fresh pair of jeans and a loose fitting sweatshirt, she topped it off with a faded ball cap and her long hair tucked up inside.

Hanging the Do Not Disturb sign on the door, she drove off into the night.

*

Deverou learned more about the history of Hawaii in three hours than he ever thought possible. Kalani was a natural teacher. She was passionate about her subject and patient with all of his questions. If he didn't understand something, she repeated it again until he did, much like a grade school teacher he once had. "Do you know her middle name?"

"I believe it's Kimberly."

"Are you sure of the spelling of her last name?"

"As far as I know it's just Day, D-A-Y. Her high school records in Salt Lake spell it that way."

"Do you have a copy of her birth certificate?"

Bert shook his head. "We never found one and we never found anyone who knew her before ninth grade."

She stacked several books on the table. "These are genealogy records for the native population here, they've been transcribed in English for all you haoles to read. I'd suggest you start going through them and looking for her last name."

"Kai, are you going to be able to stay for a while?" asked Deverou.

"I really need to work on things back at the office. When you finish here, give me a call and I'll pick you up. I can drive you through the different areas if you want," said Franklin.

"Sounds good, I'll definitely be here a while."

"The sweet rolls are getting low keiki, I think this haole has been eating too many . . ."

"I'm sure your right anakie, I'll bring some more when I come back."

Deverou took out his notebook and pen and opened the first book. It was in English, but it was written in longhand a long time ago, he knew he had a lot of hours ahead of him. By midafternoon he had been through two of the books, and found no trace of the name Day in any of the records. He was getting tired and hungry, and more than a little frustrated. Kalani brought him a sandwich and a bottle of water. "How's the search going?"

"Nothing so far, I'm beginning to think this is a waste of time," said Deverou, wishing lunch was a thick steak and a cold beer instead of a cold sandwich and water.

She sat down next to him, "I think Day is a mostly European name. The largest Asian population in the islands is Japanese and to a lesser degree, Chinese. However, about a third of the native population here has some Chinese blood in them. I suggest you try looking for a different surname or a different spelling of the name. Maybe it was changed somewhere along the way."

"That's a possibility, any suggestions on other names to try?"

"Maybe. I was looking through some old records of early farming operations and came across a couple to look at. I found Dey, Daye, Dai and Daie, they could probably all be pronounced like the European version if you wanted. Maybe her father wanted to keep it short, so it's easy to remember? It might be as good as anywhere to start."

Deverou thought about the different combinations and possibilities of names for a minute. "Kalani, I don't think her father was in the picture very much when she was young, and her mother was kind of a free spirited hippie. Maybe her mom chose an old family name from her side?"

"It's possible, do you think she just preferred the European spelling?"

Deverou shrugged his shoulders, "I don't know, but maybe she might have spelled it that way so people wouldn't be curious about it."

"I guess anything's possible, but you're really reaching here Bert."

"I don't have much else to go with. Let's follow this trail for a while and see what comes up."

"Okay then, let's start with Dai, it's on the list of possible Chinese surnames," she said, handing him two thick books. "This book has the most information about the Chinese influence in Hawaii, and this old one has a lot of the old family names and ancestry registrations from the islands."

"Can I take these with me? I suspect I will have a long night ahead of me. I'll bring them back in the morning, right after you open."

"Well, I probably shouldn't let them go out with a haole from the mainland, but go ahead and take them, but you know what it will cost you — right?"

"Uhh, no, I don't think I do . . ."

She rolled her eyes and gave him a stern look. "Sweet rolls haole — sweet rolls!"

"Oh yeah," said Deverou, with a grin, "now I remember, sweet rolls!"

*

Deverou rolled out of bed and stood up on shaky legs. He'd been up all night reading through the books she had given him. Once again, he had too much alcohol and not enough food and he sat back down quickly on the side of the bed. At least he woke up on time, that was something.

Calling Kai Franklin, he told him he would stop by the museum first, and then meet him at the office in a couple of hours. He still wanted to see some of the Asian communities.

Walking into the museum with the books under one arm and a box of fresh sweet rolls under the other, Bert poured himself a cup of coffee and waited for Kalani.

"Good morning haole! You have something for me?" she said, walking toward him with her arms open wide.

"I do, fresh from the bakery."

She hugged him for a moment then poured herself a cup of coffee. Adding a shot of flavored creamer, she opened the bakery box and put a sweet roll on her plate and reached for the jam. "So Bert, did you find anything helpful in those books?"

"A little," said Deverou, pouring himself more coffee. "I made a few notes on the name Dai, it occurred in a number of places in the ancestry registration, at least it's a place to start."

She finished another sweet roll and her coffee and put the cup and plate in the sink. After rinsing her hands she picked up a bottle of lotion, squirted some on her hands and sat back down.

Looking up from his notes he watched her rub in the cream. "What's that fragrance I smell?"

"It's just a disinfectant with a little hand lotion in it. It's called Hau Nui. It's pretty popular around here.

Hau Nui means fruity or fruitful, it smells a little like fresh melon."

Deverou felt his face flush. He realized that forensics never answered his question about disinfectants. "May I see the bottle please?"

"Sure, you need to use it on your hands?" Deverou shook his head, "No, I just want to see where it's made."

"I know where it's made, all you have to do is ask."

"Could you please tell me where it's made?"

"The Big Island, it's made on Hawaii; they grow everything down there. I think they use fruit from the area."

Holding the bottle, his hands began to shake. The label said it was manufactured in a place called Pahala, Big Island, Hawaii. After searching for more than two years, Deverou realized he was holding his first good lead in the case of Winter Day the serial killer.

"Is this stuff sold all over the islands?" "I think so, why, is that important?"

"Extremely important my Hawaiian friend, you are now my best girl and all-time favorite Hawaiian person." He bent down and kissed her on the cheek. "Thank you, thank you, thank you!"

"Hey haole, I should get something for this, right?" said Kalani, with a big grin on her face.

Deverou hugged her tight, "You know I would never forget you . . ."

*

Walking into the FBI office, he saw Kai in the hallway and motioned to meet him in the conference room.

"What's up Bert? You look happy this morning."

"If finding my first lead after more than two years of looking for this woman can't make me happy, nothing can," said Bert, unable to stop smiling.

"A new lead? That's fantastic Bert, show me what you found."

"A disinfectant that smells like melon, Kai, are you familiar with it? It's called Hau Nui."

"Maybe," said Franklin, looking at the bottle. "I think my mom may have used this stuff. I don't know too much about it, but let's see what we can find out."

Franklin had the website up in an instant and there was a postcard view of Hawaii with a bottle of their product superimposed over it. The text described how the product was an all organic, aloe based lotion scented with a mix of melon and various fruits. Originally designed to be a hand lotion, it was eventually expanded to include a disinfectant in the formula. It was made on the Big Island by a local family now in its fourth generation.

"Can we find out what their market is Kai," asked Bert. "I'd like to know if this stuff is sold on the mainland too."

Franklin nodded. "Sure, but how about we take a trip down there and see for ourselves?"

"You mean right now?"

*

The two men climbed into the helicopter. "The agency keeps a chopper to hop around the different islands, a couple of us are pilots. We're heading for Pahala, Hawaii, that's where they make the stuff."

"Sounds good to me Kai, it's a beautiful day for flying over the islands."

"I like to fly whenever I can. It's really the only way to get between the islands quickly in an emergency."

After leaving Honolulu, Deverou was enjoying the view and the history lesson Kai had been giving him. Franklin pointed out the different islands and features along the way. Deverou noticed how barren looking the island of Kahoolawe was.

"Not much on that island," said Franklin. "It's reserved for the island native's use only, no natural fresh water there. The military used it as a bombing range in World War Two."

Soon they started over the Big Island of Hawaii. "Pahala is on the south side, just outside the boundaries of Volcanoes National Park. You might have seen this area on the news over the years. It's where the lava runs over the homes and the roads. There are five different volcanoes on the island."

Deverou watched the mountains slide by as they followed the coastline. "I thought they grew lot of fruits and vegetables here?"

Franklin nodded. "They do. You'll start seeing some of the fields in a few minutes. Where it's flat enough to farm, they do well in the volcanic soil. There are also some large cattle ranches here." Turning inland, Franklin began to drop down and cross over the small town of Pahala.

After setting down at the local airport, they walked to a hangar at the end of the runway and climbed into a waiting car. "My phone says that the plant is about ten miles north of town. We should be there in a few minutes."

Walking into the lobby of the Hau Nui Company they were greeted by a pretty Polynesian girl in her late twenties, with a fresh flower in her hair. "Hi, I'm Keona, how can I help you?"

After introducing themselves and explaining why they were there, she told them she would get her father, he was the owner of the company and could help them. In a moment, a slim, gray-haired man appeared from the back and greeted them. "Hello, I'm Atiu Palakiko, how can I help the FBI today?"

"We'd like to talk about your disinfectant product if you don't mind?" said Deverou.

Palakiko nodded his head and smiled. "Certainly, that's how my family makes its living. What can I enlighten you about sir?"

Deverou opened his notebook. "Does Hau Nui sell worldwide, Mister Palakiko?"

"Oh no, not really. We've been in business for about seventy years, but it's mostly a local Hawaiian product."

"So you never send any to the mainland?"

"We do ship a little now and then, but the only way people know about it is if they tried it while they were here. We have maybe a hundred or so customers that occasionally order it from the mainland, I assumed they once lived here or visited here and liked the product."

"Atiu, can we see your shipping records for those mainland orders?" asked Franklin.

"I will have my daughter pull them up and print you a copy, is that all you need?"

"For the moment. We'll know more after we see the records, thanks," said Deverou.

"Here's the shipping records you wanted," said Keona. "Have a seat at the table if you like. Just ask if you need anything else."

"Thank you Keona, we appreciate it," said Franklin, watching her walk away.

"She is pretty, isn't she Kai?" said Deverou.

Franklin turned back to Deverou. "Yes, she is."

"Atiu was right," said Deverou. "Not that many sales outside the islands."

After going through the records of ninety-one sales shipped out of state in the last five years, they organized them into groups. The main categories were who ordered them, where were they sent and when were they sent. It only took about an hour to finish cross-referencing them with the places and dates of the Black Rose killings.

"Look at this Kai," said Deverou, pointing to his notes. "These orders were sent to four different cities where the murders occurred in the two or three months before they happened."

Franklin stared at Bert's notes for a minute. "What name did she use in Colorado?"

"Winter Day," said Deverou. "And in Albuquerque?"

"Laura Stone."

"Billings?"

"Katie Dunn."

"What about San Antonio?"

"Alexa Lewis."

"The last names match those four locations and dates of her murders," said Franklin. "All the names had a carton of six twelve ounce bottles of Hau Nui shipped to them within a few months of the crimes."

Bert leaned back in the chair and stared at the list for a minute. "W. Day had a case shipped to her in Colorado Springs about three months before the bank was robbed. K. Dunn received one in Billings and L. Stone got one in Albuquerque."

"And," said Franklin, "A. Lewis had one sent to her in San Antonio about two months before the Mexican immigrant was murdered. Jack, I think you just hit a home run here. You may have found your girl."

It's a long way to home plate, but I do think we have a good lead here, but how do we find out where she's at right now?"

Franklin slid a copy of the mail orders across the desk to Bert. "Take a look at this order, it's to an R. Roberts, in Las Vegas about three months ago."

"Vegas? I hadn't heard of a case there yet — Goddamn, she could be there now! I need to get a call in to Vegas right away."

Deverou was on the phone talking to the local agent, Matt McMahon within a couple of minutes, filling him in on the details. He went over everything they had just learned and asked if they had any similar crimes right now.

"No, not to my knowledge Bert. If she's working a casino, they tend to handle these kinds of things in house. We may never hear about a theft against them," said McMahon. "Tell me again about the tattoo part, her victims all have this black rose on their chest?"

"Yeah, on their left breast, she has one too. Can you get a memo off to the different coroners in that part of the state?" asked Deverou. "I'll send you a photo of the tattoo so everyone can see what it looks like. Matt, this is really important, she's a serial killer with a long list of victims. Make sure all the coroners understand this."

"I'm on it right now Bert. I've already sent all of them a memo, and I'll send another one as soon as I get the picture."

"Call me right away if you get anything at all. When I hang up here, I'm getting a ticket for Vegas."

"Hold on Bert, one of the other agents just got a call from Mesquite's coroner." After a pause, McMahon got back on the line. "He just read the memo and says he's had an unknown body with the black rose tattoo in his morgue for about two days."

"How'd he die?" asked Deverou. "Gunshot, head and heart."

"That's our girl, no doubt about it. I'm sending you what I think might be her last known address in Vegas. You need to check it out, but you can be sure it's been spotlessly cleaned, doubtful you'll find anything."

*

Deverou had forgotten how much he hated the sweltering heat of Las Vegas. Walking into the car rental agency he was already drenched with sweat. "We have your reservation," said the sales lady. "Any preference in model sir?"

"No, as long as it has air-conditioning."

"Here's the keys, it's a new Chevy, stall number sixty-nine."

Walking into the office, he was met by a tall lean man with close cropped hair. "Bert Deverou, I talked to you on the phone from Hawaii."

"Good to meet you Bert, I'm Matt."

"How quickly can we get to Mesquite? Have you got a chopper?"

"It's waiting at the airport right now."

The coroner's office had the body in the room when they got there. The doctor pulled back the sheet exposing his entire body. "He's dead because of the gunshots to his head and heart, but he's got nearly enough heroin in him to do the job. There's tracks in all the normal junkie places."

The tattoo was like all the others, a single black rose with a smooth stem and no thorns. Aside from that, he was rather unremarkable looking. "Matt, could he be a casino worker? Doesn't the gaming commission keep photos of all the licensed people?"

"They do. I'll get a shot of him from their facial recognition program. If he's a casino employee he'll be in there."

Deverou waited at the FBI Las Vegas office for the information from the gaming commission. He had also asked if they had a license for a female named R. Roberts. McMahon picked up his phone on the first ring, and motioned to Deverou. He pointed to his printer. They both watched as the machine spit out a picture of a man and another of a woman.

Deverou found himself staring down at a picture of a woman with her hair pulled back and black frame glasses. Winter Day stared up at him from the paper. Slightly different hair, no bangs, new glasses and different makeup, but there was no doubt — it was her. It was sharp and clear with views from the front and the profiles, something he hadn't seen before. They both were listed as employees of the Wonderland Hotel.

The hotel was just off the strip and was, at least for now, the largest hotel with the largest casino in the world. Deverou and McMahon met with the head of security, a man named Tom Fox, with the gaming commission photos. "Yeah, they did work here, but nobody has seen them for three or four days," said Fox.

"Have you had any internal robberies in the last week or so," asked Deverou.

"What makes you ask that?"

"This woman, Rachel Roberts, is a serial killer. She's done this many times before, this is as close as we've ever been to catching up to her. It's important to get on this quickly, we would really appreciate your help here."

Fox stared at the photograph for a moment. "Serial killer — her?"

"Trust me, she's as bad as they come, will you help me?"

"Agent Deverou, you know that we don't like our business aired out in public, right?"

Deverou nodded. "It will never be made public by us."

Fox picked up the photographs again. "We got hit for over two hundred thousand dollars, four days ago. These two disappeared at the same time, not much detective work needed here. We have investigators looking for them right now."

"This guy," said Deverou holding up the picture, "Josh Michaels, is on a slab in Mesquite, shot twice with a .357 magnum. The woman is in the wind, no telling where she might turn up next. I would appreciate it if you would contact me if your guys turn up anything on her."

"No problem, and if you recover our money, you'll do the same?"

"Absolutely. I'm looking for a serial killer, not a thief." Fox handed Deverou a file. "I don't know if it will help or not, but here's everything we have on the two of them."

Deverou spent the night in a small off the strip hotel. Everything he'd collected on Winter Day was scattered around the room. Sitting in the middle of the bed, he stared at the enlarged photos from the gaming commission. He remembered how striking her eyes were and how she affected all the men around her, including him.

Pouring himself a Gin and Tonic, he downed it quickly and poured another. *This really is a good drink*, thought Deverou, *a damn good drink*. Lying back on the bed holding the photo in front of him he couldn't help himself for what he was thinking about the woman in the picture. I can see what men find so attractive about you, Miss Winter Day. You are beautiful, but trust me, we are destined to meet again, and I believe it will be sooner rather than later.

Waking up with a crashing headache, Deverou made it to the bathroom before he got sick. Looking at the empty gin bottle he understood why his head hurt.

After showering and ordering coffee, he sat down in the chair and turned back to his files. He was at another dead end. He'd sent the photo and the information to every law enforcement agency in the West in the hope that someone might catch up with her.

As Deverou packed up the files he knew that his only chance to get ahead of her was to continue to follow his hunch. If things continue to go like her past history, he knew she'd be lying low for a while. He'd left Hawaii in a hurry on the news of the casino robbery. It was time to go back and keep digging. Now that he had a good photograph, someone might recognize her.

By the time Deverou got to the Honolulu International Airport he'd been awake for most of two days. On the plane he had even more drinks and by the time he reached the office he could hardly stay awake. He met Kai in the office and filled him in.

"You look like shit haole," said Kai.

"I feel even worse . . .

"Well, she is attractive," said Franklin looking at the new picture. "I can see why all those guys fell for her . . ."

"Died for her," said Deverou. "I want to get this picture out to every island and police force. I have a gut feeling that someone here knows her."

"Good as done, I've already sent one to the people at the Hau Nui store and all the different law enforcement agencies in the state are on a common mailing list. They will have their copy momentarily."

"I want to print up a bunch of these pictures in eight by ten color to show them around the heavily Asian and Polynesian neighborhoods. I need to start canvassing them as soon as possible. Oh, and I need to visit with your aunt a little more."

"I'm sure she'd be happy to see you again, you already know the price." said Franklin with a grin.

Deverou walked into the museum and saw Kalani at the counter.

"Haole! Come here and hug me . . .!"

Deverou set the sweet rolls down and she embraced him with a long crushing squeeze. "You are back, and I see you have a little gift for me?"

"A dozen sweet rolls fresh out of the oven, my Hawaiian friend."

"Thank you, thank you! You're okay, even if you are a haole . . . What can I help you with this time? You still looking for the same wahine?"

"If that means woman, then yes, I'm still looking for her," said Deverou. "However, I now have a good picture of her and I want to start showing it to the locals.

Maybe you can help me come up with the best areas to start?"

Kalani brought out a large map and rolled it out on the counter, marking several areas with a red pen. "I would probably start here," she said making an x on the map. "These are some of the oldest areas on this island. If it were me, I think maybe the schools, churches and anywhere people congregate would be a good start."

"Somehow, I don't see her as very religious, I mean she's a serial killer . . ."

"Maybe someone knows her from her earlier days here. Religion is popular here, and the biggest one is Catholic; I'd check with them and the middle schools."

Deverou was excited about being this close to his quarry but knew he had to keep things low key as he searched. He was already on thin ice with the bureau, they were on him to get this wrapped up or move on. The thought of spooking her at this late date could mean the end of his career.

*

"Thank you for your time father," said Deverou.

Looking at the photograph a second time, he shook

his head. "I'm just sorry I couldn't help. I've been here almost forty years, but she's not familiar to me."

"Are there anymore parish's that you know of that have a lot of old line families?"

"This is probably the oldest and largest on Oahu, but I can email it to the rest of the parish's if you like."

"I would appreciate that father. Please tell them if they can identify her to contact me right away, this is a very dangerous woman."

"I'll see to it Mister Deverou."

"One more question father. If you were her and wanted to hide out in Hawaii for months at a time, where would you go?"

"Well, if she has Asian and Polynesian lineage and came up in the Catholic faith, you might try Molokai. It's very beautiful and a good place to find privacy. Many people still don't like to go there because of the old leper colony, but there's been no disease there for many years."

Deverou couldn't help but wonder if this could be his last crazy shot in the dark, he was sure his bosses thought so. Molokai was even more beautiful than the old priest described. Driving around, he could appreciate this island as a great place to hide out and relax between crimes.

*

His first stop was the largest Catholic church on the island. "I'm Father Chen, what can I help you with?" Deverou found himself shaking hands with a middle aged Asian man with a thin beard and thick glasses.

Deverou handed him the wanted flyer and color photograph and explained why he was here. "Is this someone you might recognize father?"

The priest shook his head. "I don't think I've ever seen this woman before, agent."

"The flyer has her name as Day, but it's possible that it could be spelled Dai. Are you familiar with that spelling?"

"I think that there may be a few people scattered around the east part of the island with a name like that, but I rarely see them in church. You might try down along the south shore, around the old fish ponds," said Chen.

"Fish ponds?"

"They're long circles of stones built out into the water; you can't miss them."

Deverou drove the ocean highway stopping along the route to talk with locals. After an hour, a gas station attendant gave him his first positive clue. "I don't recognize her, but I know I've heard the name Dai before. I think it was around the Kupeke fishponds, a few miles east of here."

As Deverou pulled into the small village he took in the scenery for a moment. This end of the island was beautiful, with high green mountains tailing down to the ocean and small, scattered farms along the slopes.

Definitely a great place to live quietly, thought Deverou. After a quick lunch, he showed the picture to the waitress in the restaurant. She shook her head. "Never saw her before, but I have recently seen the name Dai though."

"Do you remember where?"

"I think it was in an obituary in the weekly newspaper, but I'm not positive."

Deverou felt the warm flush of excitement he always got when he thought he was closing in on his quarry. "Where can I find the local obituaries? Is there a website I can look on?"

The waitress chuckled at the idea of a website. "You're the FBI agent, look around, does it look like this place would have a website? There's only a few hundred people in the whole area."

"Do you have a Catholic church here?"

"We do," said the woman, now clearing the dishes from his table. "In fact, it's really the only church around. Everybody that wants to attend church goes there, no matter what their faith. It's half a mile down on the left."

Leaving a good tip, Deverou headed for the church. It was a small, white painted frame building with a modest steeple. An elderly priest was tending a flower bed outside when he pulled up. After introductions, Father John London invited him inside. "Let us sit and talk inside if you don't mind. It's usually much cooler in there." Pulling off his gloves and hat, he sat down in a pew. "Now, how can I help you."

Deverou explained the story to him and handed him the photograph. The priest stared at it for a minute then read the FBI flyer.

"Father, are you familiar with the name Dai?"

"Yes, there are a few people around with that name. I seem to remember doing a funeral for an elderly woman perhaps a year ago. I believe her name was Margaret."

"Is there anything else that you can tell me about her?"

"At my age, I can't remember too many details, but most people around here work small farms and gardens. A lot of them sell their produce locally."

Deverou stood up to leave, thanked the priest and walked towards the door.

"Agent Deverou . . ." "Yes?"

"You didn't ask me about the photograph."

Deverou felt another sudden rush of excitement.

"You know her?"

"As I said, memory at my age can be a bit tricky, but I think I may know who this is," said London. "When we buried Margaret there weren't many people there. She had a granddaughter if I remember correctly, I think her name was Kym. Someone told me that she had been the care giver for Margaret for years. She actually wore a black veil at the funeral, not all that common these days."

"And you're positive the woman in the picture is her?"

"I'm never really positive about anything these days agent, but If I were a betting man I'd put money on it."

"Father, this woman is extremely dangerous. For everyone's safety I would appreciate it if you didn't mention this to anyone else."

"Already forgotten."

*

Deverou checked into a tiny oceanside motel for the night. Laying out his files on the bed he made a few notes and called Kai Franklin in Honolulu. After explaining what he'd uncovered, he asked him to dig into the death certificate of a woman named Margaret, with the surname Dai from Molokai.

In minutes Franklin had the information for him. "Margaret Rae Dai, age 88, died about 11 months ago.

This looks like a pretty hot lead Bert; you need any help? I can be there in an hour."

"Not just yet Kai. It's getting too late today so I'll nose around a little more tomorrow," said Deverou. "Let me see if she's on the island right now. If she is, I don't want to tip her off by making myself known. Soon as I figure that out I'll call you. Do you have a home address for Margaret?"

"The death certificate says 1122 Puko'o Gulch Road. Keep me in the loop Bert. We already know how dangerous she is."

After a good meal, and a couple gin and tonics, Deverou fell asleep surrounded by his files. At six AM he woke up and showered, putting on a fresh shirt for the first time in days. Driving up the mountainside road, the homes were getting smaller and farther apart. Most of them were set back in the trees and appeared to be small vegetable farms.

After a long drive up the mountain, the mailboxes and house numbers began to disappear. Deverou punched in the address on his phone and found it on the map. He pulled off the road a quarter mile past the driveway and edged into the trees. Picking his way through the palms, thorns and high grass, a plain, white house came into view. Deverou sat down in the grass and pulled out his binoculars.

Next to the house was a small vegetable garden. The house was surrounded by flowers of all types and colors. As he was watching, he caught a flash of movement from inside of the house. Moving slowly on hands and knees, he crawled to within a hundred yards of the back door. Sitting against a palm tree he stared through the grass into the house. After a few minutes, he caught another flash of someone walking past the window.

In the driveway sat an older blue Jeep, splattered in mud, the only vehicle on the place. While he was watching the house, a slim figure in jeans, sweatshirt and ball cap walked out and climbed into the Jeep, in an instant it was gone. Deverou considered trying to follow but the Jeep would have too much of a head start on him.

With the Glock in his hand, he walked slowly to the house, keeping the last of the trees in front of him as cover. When he reached the door, it was unlocked and only a screen door stood in his way. Slowly pulling the handle he opened it just enough to slip inside.

He was standing in the kitchen, a tired looking room at least forty years from its last remodel. As he cleared each room he could see the house was old but very clean and organized. Judging by the contents and the furniture this was the home of an elderly person, obviously a woman.

The last room to check was a bedroom with a closed door. Stepping inside, he could see it was clearly the room of a much younger woman. Two computer screens and a large flat screen television stared out at him and everything was spotless. The clothes in the closet were neatly hung in place and every book, paper and memento were shiny clean.

On the wall above the bed was an 8 x 10 photograph of an older woman and a young, black haired girl with large dark eyes holding her hand. The room had the faint odor of melon.

Deverou's heart began to pound and his mind raced trying to sort out all of the mixed emotions he was having. He stared at the clothes in the closet and touched the computer keyboard and was startled when the screensaver popped up. It was an aerial shot of the Hawaiian volcanoes at night. He sat down on the antique brass bed, wondering what it might be like to be with this remarkable young woman, wondering how so many men could fall so hard for her.

Walking back to the kitchen he noticed a half full bottle of Bombay Sapphire Gin and two bottles of tonic water neatly placed on a towel next to the sink. Deverou couldn't resist the temptation. He found a glass and added several ice cubes. Pouring a long shot of gin he topped it off with the tonic water.

In the living room, he sat down on an overstuffed chair in the far corner. Checking the Glock one more time, he set it on the end table next to his glass, already on a neatly placed coaster. He would be right here when she returned.

The sound of a vehicle coming up the drive caused the hair on the back of his neck to stand up. He felt his face flush and his heart rate speed up. He picked up the Glock and checked it one more time, feeling the comfortable fit and lining up the sights. The screen door opened then closed with a dull thud, and Deverou sat staring at the figure in front of him. She pulled off her ball cap and let her long black hair run loose over her shoulders.

Deverou stiffened, holding the Glock squarely on center mass of the woman's body. He watched as she sat her packages down on the counter. As she turned toward him they instantly locked eyes.

"Hello Winter Day," said Bert, pointing the gun at her chest with his finger firmly on the trigger.

Her dark eyes flashed to momentary confusion, then locked onto his again. "Detective Deverou, how good to see you again."

"It's Agent Deverou, but you know that. I'm impressed with your memory Ms. Day. Just for the record tell me your real full name."

"Can I sit down first Detective? I won't be going anywhere; you've got the gun."

"Sit on the couch, right in the middle, and put these on," said Bert, tossing her the cuffs.

"Really, handcuffs? Where do you think I'm going? Like I said, you've got the gun."

He motioned for her to sit on the couch. "Do it now." Snapping on the cuffs she sat down in the middle of the couch as he directed, tucking her legs under her. Her black eyes never left him.

"Now, your full name."

"My name is Kymberly Rae Dai. My surname is spelled D-A-I, but it's pronounced D-A-Y. I was born June 20th, 1973 on the island of Molokai."

"Is Dai your father's name?"

"It's my maternal grandmother's name. That's what's on my birth certificate."

"Why did you become a serial killer?"

"You do get right to the point don't you detective."

"Answer the question."

"Here's my deal detective. I have to go to the bathroom. If you let me do that, and get a drink of water, I'll sit right here and tell you everything you want to know."

Deverou motioned with the gun for her to get up. "Leave the door open, don't make me shoot you."

"Detective, as I'm sure you already discovered, there's not a window in the bathroom, or a stash of weapons in there. There's no way for me to escape, you've got me — I'm yours."

"Stop talking and do it."

"How about these?" said Dai, holding out her cuffed wrists.

"They stay where they are."

When finished, she walked into the kitchen and got a bottle of water from the refrigerator. "I'd offer you one, but I see that you've had something already, something better than water."

"Sit down and start talking."

"I was born right here in this little house of my grandmothers. I never knew my father, and my mother moved me and my sister to the mainland when I was about eleven. She was a hippy and we ended up in Salt Lake living with one of her boyfriends. I grew up there, graduated high school and went to college there."

"Why did your mom put you in the hospital?"

"You've done your homework. She put me there because I was a pain in the ass teenager with a big IQ and nothing to do with it. I saw their shrinks, took their tests and they released me."

"When did you murder your first victim?"

"My first victim, as you call him, was in Utah, about a year before I moved to Colorado. I was working in the housekeeping department for a big hotel and my night manager kept coming on to me. After saying no several times, he cornered me in a room and raped me. Two days later I invited him into a room and stabbed him in the heart — and it felt good."

Bert was startled at her blunt admission. "It felt good . . .?"

"Detective, I have an extremely high IQ and an eidetic memory. I am also a mass confusion of sociopathic and psychopathic tendencies. I'm lacking empathy towards others or any developed sense of a conscious, at least that's what the shrinks said."

"You killed a lot of people, that doesn't bother you?"

"No."

"What about the money? You always plan a crime that gets you a lot of money."

"I had been caring for my grandmother and myself for years, she was all I had left for family. I needed money for that and it was always easy to find a man to help me get some."

"What about your mother? What happened to her?"

"I killed her."

Deverou didn't think she could shock him any more than she already had, but he was wrong.

"You killed your own mother — why?"

"She was an addict and a lost cause. Two days after my twelfth birthday she traded me to her boyfriend for drugs ."

"So she was your first victim?"

"She was not a victim, I was. I killed her in self-defense."

Deverou could hardly believe anyone was this cold. "Did you stab her too?"

"No. Stabbing was too messy; I used a gun. Detective, here's what you want to know in a nutshell. My grandmother was the only thing in my life that was good, that's why I cared for her all these years. She died about a year ago, I was her only family. Men have been coming on to me since I was in middle school. I am heterosexual and I love sex, sadly however, I hate men."

"You never had a man that you really loved?"

"I did. He cheated on me and abused me. As I see it detective, these victim's as you call them got exactly what they wanted from me. Then I took exactly what I wanted from them."

All the time they had been talking, she sat perfectly still. The riveting black eyes he remembered so well never left his. Deverou began to feel like he was being interrogated under hot lights. "Did you have to kill them when you were through with them?"

"Had I let them live I would likely have been caught a long time ago. Detective, it's very warm in here, can I change out of these long pants and sweatshirt? You can keep the gun on me the whole time, I'd like to put on shorts and a t-shirt."

Deverou was feeling flush, his palms were sweating and his heart was racing. He knew he was on dangerous ground with her. He also knew that he should have taken her in when he first confronted her.

Just like the first time they met, he felt like the upper hand was slipping away from him. But he couldn't force himself to say no, he pointed to the bedroom with the Glock. Following her into the room he unlocked one cuff, still pointing the gun at her. A black widow tattoo stared up from her from her left wrist. "Go ahead, change."

Still staring at him, she quickly pulled the sweatshirt over her head and stepped out of her jeans. "How do I look Detective? As good as you imagined?" She stood looking at him in nothing but the tiniest black lace panties and bra. Her body was smooth and tight, her light olive skin flawless. Thick black hair fell nearly to her waist.

"Here I am Detective, just like you've been dreaming about for the last two years."

She was right, he had been dreaming about this moment since they first met. "You seem pretty sure of yourself, what if I just take you to jail?"

"You won't, and we both know it. You want me. Here I am . . . I told you I like sex. Even if you take me in, we can still have a little fun."

As Deverou looked at her she ran her fingers through her hair and unhooked her bra, tossing it at his feet. She pulled back her hair slightly and showed him the black rose tattoo with the red drops of blood on the thorns. "Do you like my rose, detective?" In an instant she snapped the loose cuff on the bed post and laid back on the bed. "There detective, now I can't get away. What's the worst that could happen . . .?"

Acknowledgments

Many thanks to my family and friends for all their support . . .

Nothing much gets done in my world without help from my beautiful and talented wife, Nancy, who spends most of her time keeping me on the right track. I am a lucky man.

Thanks, as always, to my friend, book designer and photographer pal, Don Kallaus, for his talent and hard work.

Thanks to my friend Andree Le Messurier Ferguson for the killer (pun intended) original artwork for the cover. See more at: www.andreeferguson.com.

I want to thank Gary Geiser for allowing me to use his wonderful 1956, 13 seat, Valentine diner, Kings Chef, for photographs and his wonderful waitress, Savannah McDaniel, and awesome cook, Casey Bush, for making it a really fun shoot. By the way, the food is fantastic!

And to my test readers, Bob Baker, Greg Wood and Gary and Lenetta Hanes, you are invaluable to the process and much appreciated. Many thanks.

blackmulepress.com